ALIAS™

VANISHING ACT

Don't miss any of the
OFFICIAL ALIAS BOOKS
from Bantam Books

ALIAS: DECLASSIFIED
THE OFFICIAL COMPANION

THE PREQUEL SERIES

Recruited

A Secret Life

Disappeared

Sister Spy

The Pursuit/A Michael Vaughn Novel

Close Quarters/A Michael Vaughn Novel

Father Figure

Free Fall

Infiltration

Vanishing Act

And coming soon

Skin Deep

ALIAS™

VANISHING ACT

SEAN GERACE

A PREQUEL NOVEL BASED ON THE

HIT TV SHOW CREATED BY J. J. ABRAMS

BANTAM BOOKS

NEW YORK ✻ TORONTO ✻ LONDON ✻ SYDNEY ✻ AUCKLAND

Alias: Vanishing Act

A Bantam Book / July 2004
Text and cover art copyright © 2004 by Touchstone Television

ISBN: 0-553-49438-4

Visit us on the Web! www.randomhouse.com

Published simultaneously in the United States and Canada

Bantam Books is an imprint of Random House Children's Books, a
division of Random House, Inc. BANTAM BOOKS and the rooster
colophon are registered trademarks of Random House, Inc.

PRINTED IN THE UNITED STATES OF AMERICA

OPM 10 9 8 7 6 5 4 3 2 1

1

AT THIRTY-FIVE THOUSAND FEET, the Boeing 747 cut a swath through the thick cloud cover of the night sky. Inside the plane's cabin, the ceiling lights, dimmed for the late-night flight, shone unobtrusively on the magazines that sat neatly in the seat pockets. The food and beverage carts were securely stowed in the galleys, and the door locks of each lavatory read VACANT.

A lone passenger sat comfortably in a first-class seat. Her breathing was deep and mechanical, filtered through the black respiration mask that accompanied the black flight suit, helmet, boots, and goggles. On the folding tray sat a laptop computer, its screen dark.

The passenger reached forward and pushed Power. The screen brightened to show the image of a large, well-built man with a clean-shaven head that she knew only as Holcomb. He spoke with a slight Southern accent.

"Good evening, Nightwing. As we explained in your earlier brief, the prebreathe process you underwent prior to taking off was necessary for your high-altitude mission. The plane has not been pressurized, which will enable us to open the doors at this altitude without the massive decompression that would normally occur."

Holcomb hit a switch, and a digital clock readout appeared.

"Local time is 9:37 p.m."

The passenger synchronized the watch on her wrist with the display.

A moment later the door to the cockpit opened, spilling light into the cabin. A copilot, also wearing a breathing mask, stepped toward the passenger.

"We'll see you in a few minutes," Holcomb said. "Good luck."

The screen went black. The passenger turned to the copilot, who gestured for her to follow him to the stairs that led to the lower deck and then to the cargo hold. The cavernous space would normally be filled with luggage and crates, but tonight the space was empty.

At the rear of the hold, the copilot grabbed a cable from the wall and attached a clip on the end of it to a D-ring on his belt. He turned to the passenger and gave her a thumbs-up. The passenger returned the gesture and toggled a switch on the top of her helmet. There was the high-pitched whine of night-vision goggles firing up. The copilot flipped a switch on the wall. With the rumble of hydraulics, the rear cargo door descended, and in seconds the roar of the engines and the din of rushing air drowned out the sound.

The passenger checked her watch and nodded to the copilot.

The copilot nodded back.

And then the passenger—Agent Sydney Bristow—stepped to the edge of the plane and leaped out into the night sky.

*   *   *

Sydney's parachute bloomed from the backpack, a billowing, indistinguishable mass of black silk that in mere seconds snapped out to its full form. Just as planned, she touched down, almost without a sound, onto the roof of a train speeding across the landscape of Japan. The LED in her boots changed from red to green as the magnetic plates in her soles locked onto the steel surface.

Expertly she disengaged the parachute, which tumbled into the darkness. Then Sydney slid her hands into a pair of suction cups on her vest and dropped flat onto the roof of the train, her hands as well as her feet now secured. With a deep breath, she began to edge along the train top.

A tunnel yawned up ahead, and her fingers felt for a switch on her boots. *Whoosh!*

The magnetic plates deactivated and Sydney kicked both feet and rolled sideways over the roof of the train, tumbling into the space between cars just a moment before the tunnel swallowed her.

Deep inside the tunnel, Sydney slid into the cargo car, closing the door just as the train emerged. *Phew!* she thought, allowing herself to breathe again. She had trained for a mission like this, but executing it was another story. And there was zero room for a mistake.

Except for baggage, the cargo car was empty. Sydney unsnapped the chin clip on her helmet and placed it on the floor.

"Do you copy, Nightwing?" Holcomb said in her headset.

"I copy. Insertion complete."

"The clock is ticking, Nightwing. Fourteen minutes and counting."

Sydney stripped off her jumpsuit, revealing a stunning red evening gown. She tossed the jumpsuit into the corner and pulled a small case from her gear, propping it on a shelf and flipping open the hasps that secured it. Set neatly inside were a pair of long crystal earrings and a diamond brooch and ring. She grabbed the brooch—which contained a tiny hidden camera—and flicked a switch hidden on the underside. "Testing, testing," she said into the pin.

"You're good, Nightwing." Holcomb said. "Proceed."

Sydney slid the ring onto her finger and stashed her gear in the corner. Inside her handbag was a small compact. She dabbed a bit of powder on her cheeks and applied a layer of lipstick.

After pinning the brooch to her dress and putting the earrings on, Sydney reached into her bag again and pulled out what looked like a stainless-steel thermos. There was a momentary, hissing escape of pressurized air as she unscrewed the lid. She reached in and carefully pulled out a crystal champagne flute, complete with bubbling champagne.

Now the rest of her mission was about to start.

Sydney moved down the hall, no longer in

stealth, but now out in the open, just another passenger aboard the train. She crossed through the sliding doors between cars and made her way down through the first-class passenger cabins.

At the door of one of the cabins stood a man in a tuxedo. Hearing her approach, his eyes turned to her. She offered him a smile, but his gaze remained cold. He was appraising her as a threat, going through whatever list there was in his mind that provided him with the details to look for. She provided him with a no-brainer. She stumbled, tripping over one of her heels, her left arm pinwheeling for balance while her right struggled not to spill her champagne. He stepped toward her in a flash, grabbing her by the arm to stop her from falling.

"Oh, thank you *so* much," Sydney gushed. "I just can't get used to these shoes, and I'm constantly tripping." She looked up at him and smiled her best *I'm so embarrassed* smile. His eyes softened as he helped her regain her feet.

"It probably didn't help to have one of these already," she said, indicating the champagne, "but what the hey, it's a party, right?"

He smiled and nodded, letting go of her arm. Sydney saw a pistol in a shoulder holster just before his arm his slid back to his side, concealing it from view. She smiled at him again.

"Well, I better get back before I'm missed. Thanks again."

"You're welcome," he replied, and his eyes were already looking past her, surveying the hallway for someone a little more threatening than a pretty woman in a red dress who had had one too many drinks.

Sydney continued down the hall as Holcomb spoke in her ear.

"Nice work, Nightwing. I think you missed your true calling in Hollywood."

The jitters Sydney always felt before a mission were disappearing. This was a quick drop-and-pull mission, easy stuff. And the jump from the plane over the Japanese countryside had actually been fun.

Holcomb came on again. "We're at the twelve-minute mark."

Sydney crossed between cars once again. There was a considerable amount of noise coming from behind the next door.

"Ready to party?" Holcomb asked.

"Ready," Sydney said, and opened the door.

A massive party was in swing in the luxury dining cars. The room was loud and the mood fun, guests helping themselves from a lavish banquet table in the center of the car. Sydney had not eaten in hours, and her stomach noisily reminded her.

"Think you can bring me back a sandwich?" Holcomb asked.

"You wish," Sydney replied, her eyes roaming the room. "Still no sign of the target." The target was a man named Adrian Keller, an international art dealer—and thief.

"He may be in the next car. Step on over and see what we get."

Sydney crossed into the next dining car, the centerpiece of which was a decadent dessert table. She stepped over to the table to examine the delights more carefully, nodding hello to a portly man whose plate overflowed with chocolate-covered strawberries and whipped cream.

Well, Sydney thought, *I am supposed to look like one of the guests, so* . . . She took a small plate and two of the strawberries.

To think that this is how some people actually live, she mused, admiring the beautiful decorations. It was a far cry from the small dorm room she and her best friend, Francie Calfo, shared back in L.A. Although the start of their sophomore year *was* just a week away. *Maybe we'll get upgraded to that suite we requested,* she thought wistfully.

She lifted a strawberry. Her hand froze halfway to her lips. She turned toward the window, as if she were admiring the scenery going by.

"Target identified," she said under her breath.

Holcomb's voice came back in her ear. "Copy that, Nightwing."

In the reflection of the window, Sydney watched a tall man she recognized from her SD-6 briefing as Keller hold court with a couple of beautiful women. Sydney dismissed them, counting instead the five additional men in suits who flanked him.

"He has a security detail with him."

"How many?" Holcomb asked.

"Five."

Sydney assessed her options. Such a large security detail was an unexpected twist. Executives often traveled with a bodyguard, but not the veritable entourage Keller had accompanying him. Whatever he had back in his cabin, it must have been very valuable indeed.

Sydney turned and made her way across the room, her stride purposeful, confident.

Keller laughed as he shared some joke with the women. Sydney closed in, looking for an opening. Nearby, a waiter crossed the car with a tray full of champagne glasses. Sydney angled her path toward him.

Before the waiter knew what was happening, Sydney had collided with him. The tray toppled, spilling champagne on Sydney and sending the glasses cascading to the floor with a tremendous crash. She lurched forward as Adrian Keller turned toward the sound of the breaking glass. Now she bumped into him, being careful not to spill her own glass of champagne on him as his arms encircled her, catching her.

"Are you all right?" Keller asked.

Sydney feigned embarrassment.

"Yes, I'm fine," she said with a light French accent. "I'm so sorry."

"There's nothing for you to be sorry about. He should have been watching where he was going."

Sydney stepped back, dabbing at her wet dress with a cocktail napkin. "I didn't get any on you did I?" she asked.

"No, not at all." he said. He reached into his pocket, pulled out a handkerchief, and offered it to her. She wiped the champagne covering her arms.

"Thank you so much. I'd better change."

She stepped away, carefully palming the key card that she had stolen from Keller's pocket when she bumped into him.

"I have the key, proceeding to the target's suite," Sydney said, heading back down the hallway toward the luxury cabins.

"Copy that, Nightwing." Holcomb said. "We are holding at six minutes."

Sydney entered the first-class car. The guard still stood at the ready just outside Keller's cabin door. As she passed through the doorway, Sydney staggered, feigning monumental intoxication. The fact that she now reeked of expensive champagne contributed to the ruse.

This time the guard smirked when he saw her. He was clearly entertained by the notion of a repeat performance by the staggering drunken girl.

Sydney stumbled along, pretending to focus intently on not spilling any of her champagne. Then she made an obvious display of noticing the guard, standing and beaming at him.

"Hello again." She held out her champagne-soaked arms. "Look what happened. This guy totally spilled like a whole tray of champagne all over me."

The guard raised a hand to his mouth to conceal a laugh. Sydney saw it and used it. She smiled at him.

"Are you laughing at me?" She bent forward at the waist, pretending to wipe the champagne that was spilled across the front of her dress. "This is never going to come out. I might as well throw . . ."

Suddenly she jackknifed up from the waist, the top of her head catching the guard right on the chin. His head snapped back and slammed into the door behind him. His knees buckled, and he slouched against the door, stunned.

Sydney's hand flew to the top of her head, massaging the contact point.

"Ow!" she cried. *It always looked so easy on television,* she thought, *but that actually hurt!*

The guard shook his head, his eyes rapidly refocusing. His gaze fell on Sydney. His brow furrowed and his hand began to slide toward the shoulder of his jacket. Snapping back to the moment, Sydney remembered the gun hidden there.

She lashed out with her elbow, cracking the guard across the face. Unconscious, he went limp and slid to the floor.

Sydney pulled the guard's gun from his shoulder holster. It was a full-size nine-millimeter, large for her small, delicate hands, but she expertly ejected and checked the clip before slamming it back into the handle.

Then she reached into her purse, pulled out the key card, and slid it into the lock. There was a click, and an indicator light above the door glowed green. With the guard's weight leaning against it, the door flew open faster than she expected. She reached out to catch the door handle but missed. The guard fell back into the room and his head hit the floor with a thud.

"Ooh, sorry," she said, wincing. If he hadn't had a concussion before, he certainly did now.

Sydney glanced down at her watch. Time was getting very short. She couldn't leave the guard in the hallway. In one hand she held the champagne glass; in the other, the gun. Quickly she stuck the gun into her tiny shoulder purse, with the handle sticking out the top. She stepped into the room, grabbed the guard by his collar, and dragged him into the cabin, shutting the door behind her with the toe of her shoe.

She spoke into her microphone. "I'm in the target's room."

"Copy that, Nightwing." Holcomb replied. "Let's shake and bake."

Sydney dropped her purse onto the bed. The gun flopped out and fell onto the floor. She'd retrieve it in a minute—right now she had to find . . .

Jackpot. She pulled a battered metal box from underneath the bed and hoisted it onto the mattress.

"I found the package, opening it now."

She reached up and pulled off one of her crystal earrings. She dipped the earring into the champagne and, squeezing the tiny bulb hidden at the top, extracted some of the champagne into the delicate crystal tube.

Now Sydney squeezed some of the champagne—which was actually a highly concentrated acid compound concocted by Graham Flinkman back at SD-6 in L.A.—onto the two locks on either side of the case. With an abrupt hiss, accompanied by wisps of smoke, the acid began to eat through the metal. In seconds the locks were eroded. Sydney dropped the earring into the glass and opened the case.

Inside was a very old iron key. It was easily the size of her hand, and was covered with elaborate etchings and markings. Sydney reached with delicate fingers and pulled the key from the case, staring at it with a sense of awe until Holcomb abruptly cut in on her earpiece.

"Nightwing, you have been compromised. The target is en route to your location." When Sydney had taken Adrian Keller's card key, she had slipped a tiny transmitter into his pocket so that Holcomb could track him.

"Copy that," Sydney said, her pulse speeding up. "Heading to cargo."

As Sydney stepped to the door, Holcomb suddenly shouted over her earpiece. "Negative! They are in the hallway and moving toward you."

Sydney knew that in moments men with guns

would be storming through the door. She had to stall them . . . but how?

She looked around the room. None of the furniture was bulky enough to create any kind of obstacle. The guard still lay unconscious. Her eyes fell on the metal box with its burned locks.

She scooped up the glass of acid and poured it into the electronic lock of the door. A shower of sparks spilled from the lock and the green light went out. She gripped the door handle and pulled. The door was secured.

Great, now they can't get in, she thought, relieved. *But how am I going to get out?* She looked around the room, searching for some kind of a miracle.

She ran to a closed door and opened it. A closet. Another one: the bathroom, complete with a shower stall hanging open. She caught a reflection of herself in the mirror over the sink. She was startled by how pale, how scared she looked.

Sydney blinked, her eyes flickering with an idea. "Holcomb! Give me room schematics, quick!"

2

THE ROOM WAS EMPTY.

Not a word was spoken by Adrian Keller or his guards, their communication limited to a series of military hand signals, their unique language of uncover and discover.

A round of gunfire had released the door with the melted lock. Now, at Keller's behest, one of the guards advanced toward the closed bathroom door and kicked it open. It splintered at the force of his kick, and snapped off its hinges, falling to the floor with a crash.

Before the door had even hit the floor, two of the guards were stepping into the bathroom, guns raised.

One of the guards eased toward the curtain and looked back at his partner, who nodded.

The guard ripped the curtain open. The stall was empty.

Keller shoved his way past the guards in the main cabin, pausing only when he saw the empty metal box lying on the bed, smoke coming from the burned locks.

"She has the key," he said in a boiling mix of rage and panic. One of the guards stepped out of the bathroom.

"It's empty."

Keller spun toward him, his hands gripped into fists.

"The door was locked from the inside." He pointed to the unconscious guard on the floor. "He certainly didn't do it, and she couldn't have just vanished into thin air. Where did she go?"

The lights flickered as the train rumbled over a rough patch of track. Light suddenly spilled out of the bathroom.

They all turned to see the vanity mirror over the sink swinging open. One of the guards ran to the opening and peered inside. Instead of shelves, he saw the bathroom in the cabin next door, its floor littered with the shattered remains of the vanity.

One of the guards ran out into the hallway. The door of the next cabin stood wide open. He ran back into the room.

"She's gone."

* * *

After she had kicked through the vanity shelf and crossed over into the next cabin, Sydney sped down the hall toward the cargo car. Holcomb was coaching her in the earpiece.

"Does the train have a security system that we can hack into, something with cameras that can help us?" she asked, clutching the key.

"Negative. We're wearing blinders on this one. Just move quickly and get out of there."

Sydney pulled open the cargo door and was about to step through when she stopped. She reached down and plucked the brooch from her dress. She stuck it into the frame of the door, turning it so that the camera inside was aimed down the hall.

Holcomb's voice was so ecstatic she almost smiled.

"Good idea, Nightwing, now we've got your back. Let's get a move on, we're almost out of time."

Sydney ran into the cargo hold, moving quickly past the racks of luggage to one of the massive sliding doors on the side of the car. She reached for the handle, and her fingers clutched the cold steel. She began to pull, but then slowly, her fingers released the handle. She reached down and grabbed the shiny padlock that secured the door.

It was locked. Sydney would have to shoot it off. There was only one problem.

Her gun was on the floor—in Adrian Keller's room.

*   *   *

The guard paused outside the cargo door, listening intently for any sound that would betray an occupant. The room was silent.

Abruptly he ripped the door open, and a shaft of light pierced the shadows. He quickly stepped into the room, heading toward the shadows. He pulled a small flashlight from an inner pocket of his coat and clicked it on, sweeping light over the room in a slow arc.

He had thought for sure that the girl had come

this way. He turned to give the room one more look, the beam of his flashlight stripping the dark away from the numerous carts and boxes filling the room.

The light fell on a small bundle shoved between boxes. He stepped forward.

Stashed in the space were a black jump helmet and a backpack. He kneeled down beside the backpack, stirring through the contents with the muzzle of his gun.

He pulled a small walkie-talkie out of his pocket. "I found something in cargo. You better come check it out."

He placed his gun on the floor and continued to rummage through the bag, oblivious of the fact that, directly above him, Sydney Bristow hung precariously from the ceiling, held in place by the suction cup hand grips she had used to board the train.

* * *

Sydney stared at the ceiling and tried to ignore the pain in her arms. She had quickly climbed into her flight suit and run the safety straps from the suction cups underneath her back as a makeshift harness. The key lay heavily in her pocket.

She could hear the guard below her going through her bag. When he had entered the car, she was sure that he would see her, but in the darkness her black suit had kept her out of his sight.

She turned her head slightly and looked down. Her eyes immediately seized on the gun that rested beside the guard on the floor, just out of her reach. *How could I have forgotten my gun?* she moaned inwardly. The pain in her arms was getting monumentally worse with every passing second. She wondered what chance she would have if she dropped on him now, using the element of surprise, and hopefully *his* gun, before he knew what was happening. And she knew there was more trouble on the way. He had called for assistance, and there would be more guards walking through the door at any moment. As she considered the possibilities, things suddenly got far worse.

Holcomb came on over the radio. "Nightwing, do you copy? What's your status?"

Sydney's mouth went dry as she heard the same transmission bleed out over the guard's radio. She watched in horror as he picked up his handset. Holcomb repeated his questions, with intermittent bursts of static. And again his words emitted from the guard's radio. The guard started to adjust his controls and then stopped. And Sydney knew what he was thinking. *Signals cross only when the radios are close to one another.*

In a flash he drew his flashlight again and swept the corners of the room, his other hand gripping the radio. *He knows I'm nearby!*

When Holcomb repeated his message again, Sydney's earpiece delivered a drilling high-pitched squeal. She gasped as her teeth rattled under the assault.

The guard froze, hearing the noise, and raised his flashlight toward her. Without another option, she was forced to release the pressure on the suction cups and drop to the floor.

Sydney landed in a crouched stance and sprang, catching the guard by surprise. He reached for his gun and she kicked it, sending it skittering across the floor.

She snapped out a punch, completely forgetting about the mechanical mitts covering her hands. The blow caught the guard's nose, drawing blood and his fury.

His leg shot out, catching her in the midsection, knocking the wind out of her and sending her flailing back against the wall. She caught herself with her hands, cushioning her impact. She moved to reengage him but was trapped by the suction cups, which had activated, pinning her to the wall. He moved in on her, fists drawn back.

As he punched, Sydney disengaged the cups.

She rolled forward in a somersault, springing to her feet a moment later. The harness cables dangled from the suction cups.

The guard adjusted quickly and snapped a jab at her head. She kicked, catching him in the ribs. Momentarily stunned, he paused for a second, and that was all Sydney needed.

She sidestepped, snaring his arm in the cable and twisting it back over his head. She clamped the suction cup to the wall, securing his arm. Clueless as to what was happening, the guard reached for her, only to discover that his arm was trapped. Sydney took advantage of his momentary confusion and secured his other arm to the wall the same way, effectively pinning him to the wall, then snapping off the disengaging switch so there was no way he could free himself. He struggled against his bonds, but the cups held fast.

Sydney grabbed the gun off the floor. The guard stopped struggling, his eyes betraying his fear as Sydney clicked the safety off.

She blew a strand of hair from her eyes and wiped the sweat from her brow with the back of her hand. She raised the gun and blew the padlock off the side door. Her ears rang from the reports that echoed in the silence that followed.

Sliding her sleeve down over her fingers, she

plucked the smoking lock from the door catch. Then she dropped the smoldering hunk of metal to the floor and pulled open the door.

The cargo car was immediately filled with the noise of the train and the air rushing past. The landscape blurred, vaguely aglow with the moonlight that had finally broken through the clouds.

Sydney could hear Holcomb in her ear, but his words were lost in the roar. She clasped her hands over her ears and asked him to repeat what he had said. His voice came back loud and strong, and Sydney felt her knees weaken.

"The guards are coming through the door! Repeat, the guards are—"

The door behind her opened, and Sydney turned in time to make eye contact with the first guard entering the cabin. He raised his gun, but Sydney drew faster, and fired. Bullets pinged off the floor around the guard's feet, and he retreated into the hallway.

Sydney's training had taught her to fire in controlled bursts designed to conserve ammo, but panic took over, and she fired and fired until the gun clicked empty.

The guards flooded into the room, guns trained on her.

"Drop your weapon!" one of them screamed.

Sydney let the gun fall from her hands. It banged heavily on the floor, and she winced at the noise despite the voices that overwhelmed her as the guards each barked orders at her.

"Get on your knees!"

"Put your hands behind your head!"

"Get down!"

"Now! Now!"

Sydney laced her fingers behind her head and dropped to her knees.

The guards moved in for the inevitable kill. Then they stopped, looking outside as, impossibly, a second train pulled up alongside.

Holcomb stood at the open door of the second car. He leveled a machine gun and fired.

Sydney fell to the floor and rolled to her right as the cargo car was suddenly lit up with the strobelike flicker of the machine gun's muzzle flash. A luggage rack beside the guards was splintered into thousands of pieces under the assault of the gun. The guards fled back into the hallway once again.

"Come on!" Holcomb roared, and Sydney was on her feet in a flash, the stolen key now gripped tightly in her hand.

Sydney ran for the open door, and for the

second time in twenty minutes, leaped out into space. She sailed across the abyss through the cold, rushing wind.

Everything slowed down, the world moving in slow motion. Sydney felt her senses pushed to the limit with adrenaline. Over the roar of the open air she could hear her heartbeat pounding in her ears. She saw Holcomb, wide eyed; she saw the agents in the tiny room behind him looking at her with utter disbelief.

And then she began to fall. *I'm not going to make it.* She was going to fall beneath the spinning wheels of the train. She was going to die.

In the space of a heartbeat her tears began, dried by the wind before they could cross her cheeks. She closed her eyes and waited for the end.

She jerked as three pairs of hands snagged her jumpsuit. Her teeth snapped together with a jaw-rattling click, and her eyes flew open, staring into the strained faces of Holcomb and his colleagues.

"Pull!" Holcomb screamed, and the three of them hauled Sydney into the safety of the car. She landed hard on her back, the wind momentarily knocked out of her. The key popped out of her hand and struck the floor. An agent caught it on one bounce.

"You're all right," Holcomb said, and Sydney

looked up into his smiling face. The adrenaline suddenly left her, and the world began to fade. She took one last look outside.

In the open door of the train she had just fled stood Adrian Keller, staring at her with burning eyes. Then the tracks split, carrying him away into the night.

And Sydney passed out.

3

"AND IF IT WASN'T bad enough that they lost my reservation, they lost my luggage in Seattle. I asked them to explain how they could lose my luggage in Seattle when I was in Chicago." Sydney sighed. She'd had to make up a story about attending a distant cousin's wedding. It had been just a year since she had joined SD-6, and already Sydney felt as if she had given Francie every excuse in the book.

Francie shook her head. "See, that is why I never check luggage. Anything I can't fit into an overnight bag is not that important to bring along. Right, Tim?"

The six-year-old on her lap giggled and shook his head.

"No!" Francie exclaimed in mock exasperation. "What do you mean, no?" She tickled him in his side, and he burst into gales of infectious laughter, kicking his orange-sneaker-clad feet in the air.

Sydney laughed and took another bite of her pizza. It wasn't the best pizza in the world, but this was Pizza Parade, after all, known more for its kids' games and rides than for its food.

Francie suddenly stopped tickling Tim and looked around at the dozens of kids amped up on sugar running pell-mell around the place. "Hey, have you seen Erica?"

Sydney nodded, her mouth full of pizza, and pointed to the adorable little girl with blond pigtails who was laughing and dancing around in the center of a pit filled with multicolored plastic balls.

Francie let out a sigh of relief as Tim joined in the fray again. "I should really put all that energy to use. We could hire them to clean our dorm room. Or help us move into that suite, if we're lucky enough to win the housing lottery. Or go grab us coffee from Starbucks."

Sydney laughed. "See, that's why they created child labor laws." She took a sip of her soda. "You're really liking this nanny job, aren't you."

Francie made a silly face, then smiled. "You know, I can actually say that I'm going to miss them when school starts next week. And that's not something I saw coming at the beginning of this summer."

Sydney sat back in her seat. She still couldn't believe that in a few days she'd be back in class, this time as a sophomore. Her freshman year at UCLA had gone by in a blur of books and friends . . . and training and missions.

"Of course, I can still watch them if they need a sitter sometimes, but it's not like I'm going to be around them twenty-four seven. It's just . . ." Francie stopped, suddenly craning her neck as she looked for Erica.

"She's on the jungle gym."

Francie turned back to her. "So is there any chance you're going to change your mind about coming with us this weekend? The dorm room can wait, you know. And so can the bank." A group of people from their dorm were going to Vegas for the long weekend, and Francie had been pestering Sydney for days to go with them.

But after having most of the month of August off from Credit Dauphine—a gift of sorts from Sloane after the draining emotional mission she had gone on to Russia back in July—things were definitely heating up again at SD-6, as evidenced by her recent trip to Japan. Now that it was September, Sydney thought it best to keep herself available. Just in case duty called, she wanted to be ready to answer.

As if on cue, Sydney's pager went off. Francie shook her head.

"See, I did that. I jinxed it. If I hadn't said anything about work . . ."

Sydney checked the pager. The display read SLOANE. She looked up at Francie, who rolled her eyes.

"I know, I know, you have to go."

Sydney shrugged apologetically. "Sorry."

Francie nodded. "I know. But hey, I'm glad you could have lunch with us."

"Me too." Sydney tossed her napkin down on the table and gave Francie a wave good-bye. Somehow she had a feeling that Vegas was going to have to wait.

* * *

Wearing a black pantsuit, her long hair pulled back in a no-nonsense ponytail, Sydney strode through the narrow corridors of SD-6 toward the main conference room.

As she neared the door, she could see Arvin Sloane through the windows, handing out mission folders. She felt butterflies take flight in her stomach. For some reason she felt an almost desperate need to impress this man, even more than she had with Wilson, her first handler at SD-6.

Perhaps she was imagining it, but Sloane seemed very concerned about Sydney's well-being, confident in her abilities but making sure she wasn't taking on more than she could handle. His manner with her was almost . . . paternal.

She shook her head, not at the idea of Arvin Sloane's treating her like a daughter but at the reminder of Jack Bristow, the cold, uncaring man who was her father. Sloane cared, and it was a welcome change. She tried to erase the thoughts of her father from her mind as she opened the door and stepped into the conference room. Several other SD-6 agents sat at the table.

"Thank you for coming in on such short notice, Sydney." Sloane said, "And let me be the first to congratulate you on a mission well done." He turned to address the room. "Thanks to Agent Bristow's efforts in Japan, we were able to obtain a significant piece of an emerging black market puzzle."

Sydney took a seat and opened the folder in front of her as Sloane retrieved a remote control from the table. He turned to the large screen over the table and tapped a button. The overhead lights dimmed slightly as the screen lit up, displaying a surveillance photo of Adrian Keller.

"Adrian Keller." Sloane continued. "A world-renowned art dealer who specializes in the acquisition and restoration of priceless works of art. Some of you may remember him from the article in *Smithsonian* that chronicled his restoration of the entire Polan family collection in Versailles.

"What was conspicuously left out of the article is the fact that Mr. Keller has also been suspected of participating in a number of high-profile thefts and forgeries."

Sloane tapped another key on the remote. A photograph of the key Sydney had retrieved was displayed.

"This was recovered by Agent Bristow and a special team just days ago. At this point Research still hasn't been able to discern its purpose. What we do know, however, is this."

He hit another button, and a stern-looking man stared out at them with cold, calculating eyes.

"The key was destined for this man: Viktor Romero. An international arms dealer who has been linked to countless terrorist acts against the United States and its allies.

"As I said, we have no information on the key, with the exception of a transmission we intercepted that included a Latin word meaning magic. As it happens, Mr. Romero has been working as a stage manager for Trevor Raven."

Trevor Raven? Sydney and Francie had watched one of his TV specials last winter. He was a famous—and very handsome—illusionist.

"Our best guess is that Romero has been using Trevor Raven's recent world tour as a cover to transport arms across the borders of the countries on the tour."

"Does Raven know about this?" Sydney asked, looking down at her folder.

"It doesn't seem so. He appears to be an innocent pawn in this whole affair. But we may have an opportunity to dismantle Romero's work.

"Last week one of the stage assistants in the show broke her arm. The tour was postponed, and in two weeks they will be having auditions in London for her replacement."

Sydney felt a tingle of excitement and stopped reading the report. She looked up at Sloane.

He was looking right at her.

"Agent Bristow, you will travel to London to participate in the auditions and secure a position on the stage team, thereby allowing you to monitor Viktor and report your findings to us."

Sydney stared at Sloane in disbelief. "But what if I don't pass the audition?"

Sloane met her eyes again, and a smile, true and strong, crept in at the corners of his mouth. "I have faith that you will. If you can accomplish all that you have so far in such a short period of time, I have no doubt that you can succeed with this.

"In addition, we have set up a special training schedule to prepare you for the audition. For the next two weeks, you will meet with a contact that we have at the Magic Castle in Hollywood, and he will put you through the paces required for performing in a major stage show."

He turned off the monitors. "That will be all."

Everyone rose from their chairs, taking the mission folders with them as they left. Sydney paused at the door and turned to Sloane, who was gathering his things.

"Mr. Sloane," she said uncertainly, "I have classes that begin—"

He raised a hand, and she stopped. He gestured to a chair, and she took a seat. He pulled out the chair nearest to her and sat facing her.

"Agent Bristow, I know that you have doubts.

Doubts about the mission, which, in turn, raise further questions in your mind about your abilities to serve this agency. In truth, if you didn't, we would be worried. It is doubt that allows us to evaluate our abilities in a realistic way, free of the arrogance and overconfidence of thinking that you know everything.

"Now, with that in mind, I'm sure you can understand that SD-6 is not in the business of putting agents in situations of unnecessary risk, because that jeopardizes not only the life of the agent in question, but the lives of their fellow agents, and ultimately, our country."

Sydney nodded, feeling the weight of it all, and looked down at the floor, her hands clutching at the folder on her lap. "Yes, but—"

"Sydney," Sloane said. He reached forward and placed a hand over her hers. "Your professors will make an exception for you. We've worked everything out." He smiled. "You're here, right where you are now, because you have extraordinary talent and abilities. You have barely begun to even scratch the surface of what you're capable of. I have been in this business for many years, and never, in all that time, have we encountered someone like you."

He patted her hand. "It's almost as if you were born to do this."

She gave him a smile, briefly, before the furrowing of her brow drove it away. She reached up and brushed an errant strand of hair behind her ear, shaking her head as her fingers brushed against her temple.

"I can't believe what I've accomplished this past year," she confided, her eyes rising to meet his.

Sloane smiled and squeezed her hand reassuringly. "I can," he said. "And I think you know that this is just the beginning. Despite all the doubt, the self-criticism, you know, in the back of your mind, that you're good at this. You just have to start believing it."

He smiled at her and continued. "Because we already do."

4

ON HOLLYWOOD BOULEVARD, TOURISTS milled in endless circles in front of the Chinese Theatre, searching for the names of their heroes etched forever in concrete. Occasionally they would stop and raise cameras that in a flash would capture the proof they would show their friends back home, or they would kneel and place their hands within the prints of the silver-screen stars, often awed that these giants of entertainment had such small hands.

A block over on Franklin Avenue, under the watchful eye of the Hollywood sign, stood the

Magic Castle, a private club whose members were drawn by a love of the magical arts.

Its narrow tree-lined driveway was host to a parade of luxury automobiles that wound their way up the hill to the main entrance. Valets in red jackets opened car doors for men in suits and the women in elegant eveningwear who stepped from their cars and walked through the front door of the Victorian mansion.

A valet stepped to a gleaming silver Mercedes and opened the driver's door, extending a hand to Sydney. She took it and stepped from the car, leaving the keys in the ignition. Then she tucked her purse under her arm and entered the club.

Sydney made her way to the Grand Salon bar and took a seat at a small table in a corner. After a moment, a waiter appeared to take her order. She ordered a Diet Coke, and the waiter vanished as quickly as he had appeared.

She reached into her purse and pulled out a compact, snapped it open, and checked her makeup in the mirror. A man appeared at her shoulder, reflected in the glass.

"Pick a card," he said.

Sydney turned in her chair to face him. Circular wire-rimmed glasses were perched precariously at the end of his narrow nose, and he had a bushy full beard. His hands deftly shuffled a deck of cards, their twisting dance accompanied by the whisper of their edges snapping delicately from his fingertips. He smiled and fanned out the deck facedown. "Come on, pick a card."

She returned his smile and looked down at the cards. She reached for one, hesitated, and picked another, hiding its face from him.

"Okay," he said, "memorize the card."

Sydney turned the card over so only she could see it. The card was a seven of clubs. She looked up at him and nodded.

He continued on. "Now put the card back in the deck." Sydney slid the card back into the deck, and almost instantaneously his fingers were working their magic again, shuffling the cards once, twice, three times.

He fanned the cards out as before, widening the spaces between them until he revealed a single card from the deck that was faceup. It was the seven of clubs.

His eyes twinkled as they undoubtedly had a million times before, waiting for the shocked look on the person's face as he revealed the card.

"Is that your card?"

Sydney looked up at him, shock in her eyes, but then she shook her head. The smile faltered on the magician's face, his twinkling eyes blinked.

"No?" he asked incredulously.

"I'm sorry, but that wasn't my card," Sydney said almost sheepishly. The magician scratched his head, puzzled at his failure. He looked at her over the rim of his glasses.

"You mind telling me what card it was?" he asked.

Sydney smiled. "It was the two of hearts."

"Of course," he said, shaking his head. "The two of hearts."

He winked at her, and she nodded in return, acknowledging the exchange of code phrases that had passed between them.

He bowed at the waist, in what appeared to be a gesture of gratitude to those at the surrounding tables, but as he bowed he leaned in and whispered to Sydney.

"Nice to meet you, Agent Bristow. My name is Garret Pinsky. Wait until I leave, and then meet me in the hall outside the Palace of Mystery." He turned and walked away, slipping out onto the hallway.

Sydney took a drink from her glass and set it

back on the table. Then she tucked her purse under her arm, and slid from her chair, gliding gracefully across the room and out the door.

Pinsky stood at the end of the hall in front of a pair of doors beneath a sign that read, in elaborate gold letters, THE PALACE OF MYSTERY. She walked down the hall toward him. As she neared, she saw there was an additional sign tacked to the door that read CLOSED FOR RENOVATIONS.

Pinsky reached into the pocket of his suit jacket and produced a key. Checking to see that no one was watching, he slid the key into the lock.

Sydney stepped inside, her shadow thrown ahead of her by the lights in the hall. Pinsky followed and closed the door, sealing them in the dark.

Pinsky hit a hidden switch and the house lights came up, revealing the luxurious interior of the theater.

"The Palace of Mystery is the largest of the three main showrooms in the castle," Pinsky explained, making his way down the center aisle toward the stage. "The Close-up Gallery, which is the smallest of the theaters, is for close-up magic."

Sydney followed Pinsky down the aisle, admiring the beauty of theatre.

"Then there's the Parlour of Prestidigitation,

which recreates the Victorian experience of the living room, or parlor, magician."

He stopped in the center of the aisle and raised him arms to the space around him. "The Palace of Mystery hosts the grand-illusion performances. This is where we'll be for the next two weeks. Each of the theaters here undergoes annual restoration and redecorating, so no one will be suspicious of this theater's being closed for an extended period of time."

Pinsky stepped up the stairs leading to the stage and Sydney followed. She turned and looked out at the rows of empty seats.

So this is what I'm getting myself into, she thought. She tried to recall if she had ever gotten stage fright. She turned back to Pinsky, who was simply staring at her, hands folded across his stomach.

"Do you have any questions before we start?" he asked.

Sydney shook her head.

He clapped once, and the sound echoed around the massive room. "Then let's begin. We've got a good amount of information to cover in the next two weeks. But first, one thing."

He rolled up his sleeves, exposing his forearms,

and started rubbing his hands together in brisk circles. After a moment he opened his hands, and there nestled in one palm was a single red rose. He offered it to Sydney.

"A rose for the lady, for good luck." He winked, his smile wide. Sydney laughed and took the rose. And they began.

* * *

For the next two weeks Pinsky taught Sydney the skills of an accomplished stage assistant. Every night after classes she told Francie, in the middle of an all-out campaign to snag a bigger room, she was off to the library, then went to the Magic Castle in a completely different disguise, giving her an opportunity to practice a series of radically different looks and personas.

By the end of her training, Sydney had learned enough of the craft of stage magic to perform in a major show. Her final test was to perform alongside Pinsky in the opening performance in the "newly redecorated" Palace of Mystery. Sydney was amazed by how much fun she had, and was even more thrilled by how much she enjoyed the applause and the excitement of it all.

After the show, there was a knock at her dressing room door. Sydney opened it to find Pinsky standing there, still dressed in his coat and tails. He held a flat black disk in his hand.

"Sydney I just wanted to tell you how great you were tonight. I'm very proud of you," Pinsky said.

Sydney blushed at the compliment. "Thank you."

"I guess I should be proud of myself as well," Pinsky continued. He smiled and shrugged. "After all, I taught you everything you know."

Sydney laughed and nodded. "Yes, you did. You taught me everything you know."

He smiled and shook a finger at her. "Uh-uh, not so fast. I said I taught you everything *you* know, not everything *I* know." He winked at her. "I still have a trick or two up my sleeve."

He held the disk out and snapped his wrist. The disk popped out to a full top hat. As Sydney watched, he reached into the hat and pulled out a small wrapped box.

Sydney blinked at the display of close-up magic. Pinsky bowed and held the box out to her.

"This is to congratulate you on a job well done. You were wonderful tonight, and I know you'll wow them on the mission."

Sydney unwrapped the box and opened the lid. Inside was a beautiful silver chain with a coin-sized medallion pendant.

Sydney gasped. Carefully, she took the pendant from its bed of white tissue, its delicate chain swinging from her fingertips. "It's so beautiful. Thank you so much."

"Not at all, Sydney. It's I who should thank you. You have been a wonderful pupil." He gestured to the pendant. "May I?"

Sydney held her hand out, and he plucked the pendant from her palm. He held it by the chain, and the pendant swung back and forth while he spoke.

"I bought this many, many years ago in Milan, when I was traveling through Europe and just starting out as a magician. It has been with me on many journeys all over the world. Now my traveling is done, so I give it to you. I hope it brings you the same good luck and fortune that it brought me."

He began to give it back to her and stopped short. "Oh, there's one more thing. Watch."

With delicate fingers he pressed the medallion. It slid open to reveal a small compartment.

"Perhaps this will come in handy for you someday," he said.

5

SYDNEY WALKED DOWN THE hall at SD-6, striding purposefully toward Sloane's office. It was time for her final prep meeting before she caught a plane for London.

As she rounded a corner, she stopped suddenly. At the end of the corridor, going over the contents of a mission folder with another agent, was . . . someone who looked like Noah Hicks.

It had been two weeks since she had seen Noah, at dinner in a small bistro in Santa Barbara. Noah, as cautious as ever, had felt that it would be a good idea to have dinner together as far from Los Angeles as they could manage. They had sat at a quiet table for two that looked out over the ocean, far removed from the noise and congestion of the city.

On the drive back along the Pacific Coast Highway in Noah's vintage car, Sydney watched as the sun dipped and kissed the ocean, the sky glowing in shades of red. She was momentarily startled as Noah grabbed her hand, entwining his fingers with hers. She turned toward him and his eyes, momentarily taken from the road, stared into hers. He raised her hand to his lips and kissed it gently, his lips brushing against the back of her hand. She had then slid across the seat toward him, cradling their hands against her stomach, and rested her head on his shoulder. She had dozed then, thinking there was no place she'd rather be.

Two days later he went on a mission, and she hadn't seen him since.

She was abruptly torn from her reverie when another agent bumped into her as he came around the corner behind her. The mission folder dropped from her hand, and before she could move to retrieve it, the agent bent down and scooped it from the floor.

His eyes were apologetic as he handed the folder back to her. "Sorry about that," he said.

"No, I'm sorry," Sydney said. "I shouldn't be standing in the middle of the hallway."

The agent smiled and put a reassuring hand on her arm. "That's all right," he said. He held up his own mission folder as if it had all the answers, backing away as he continued.

"I'm late. You take care." He smiled, waved, and was gone, lost in the parade of agents that bustled by.

Sydney liked him, had met him once before. *What was his name?* she asked herself as she resumed her walk toward Sloane's office. *Dixon, that was it. Marcus Dixon. I hope we get to work together someday.*

* * *

Sydney had left SD-6 as Special Agent Sydney Bristow, but she had arrived at LAX as Nicole Bennet, aspiring actress and magician's assistant. She boarded the plane using identification freshly manufactured by SD-6. In her suitcase she had an envelope of head shots and resumes that she would bring to the audition. The resume was modest, yet portrayed a determined and rising talent. Each reference was carefully crafted to provide impeccable credentials. All Sydney had to do was play the part.

When the plane finally arrived at Heathrow, a light rain was falling, and every wet surface of the city shimmered with broken light. Sydney collected her bags and hailed a cab from curbside, directing the driver to take her to her hotel.

As the cab maneuvered through early-morning London traffic, her sprits brightened. She loved London, a city rich with history, and hoped she would have a chance to sightsee. But she also realized that she would have all the time in the world to go sightseeing if she didn't pass the audition. Until then, she had better focus on the task at hand.

The cab pulled up to the hotel, a small economy place that fit the profile of her resume. The driver retrieved her bags from the trunk. Sydney paid him, then stepped through the front door of the hotel.

The room was small, with sparse furnishings, a perfect place for someone trying to enjoy Europe on a shoestring. Sydney didn't bother to unpack but sat down on the bed and began to review her mission folder.

As she glanced over the pages, the smells of breakfast, most likely from the small restaurant downstairs, drifted to her and her stomach growled. Her audition was in three hours, so she didn't want a big meal. But she hadn't eaten much on the plane, and who knew how long the auditions would take? *A little snack will give me just the energy I need.*

She went down to the restaurant, purchased a muffin and an orange juice, and took them back up to her room. After she had eaten, she dozed off on the bed, the mission folder open on her lap. She awoke an hour later, refreshed and ready to go. She washed her face and brushed her teeth, grabbed her bag, and set out for the audition.

As the cab pulled up to the theater, where the auditions were being held, Sydney realized that she had no idea what to expect when she went through the doors. She wondered how many people there would be trying out for a single, coveted position.

Pushing through the revolving door, she found her answer. A group of about thirty girls milled around the spacious lobby, their head shots in hand.

"Oh, wow," Sydney said, not realizing she had said it aloud. She had spent so much time concentrating on the details of the mission that she had not really thought about the first and most important step: the audition.

There was a small table near the revolving doors. With numb fingers, Sydney wrote Nicole Bennet on the blank line beneath the many names already scribbled on the sign-in sheet.

She wandered over to a nearby water fountain, her eyes surveying the girls around her, and took a drink. After a moment she stood, her throat still dry despite the water, and took a seat on the flight of marble stairs that ascended to the balcony.

I hope two weeks of training were enough, she thought. There were so many people here, and even now a couple more were entering through the revolving doors. Sydney felt a headache begin to drum at her temples, and she massaged it away with her fingertips.

I have to relax, she told herself. *This is not the time to get all worked up.* Her fingers still pressing at her temples, Sydney closed her eyes. Her mind drifted back to the Magic Castle and Pinsky. At first it had been difficult, as all new things usually are. But as the training had progressed, it had become more and more fun as she quickly adapted and learned everything with ease. She had learned from the best, during an intense and accelerated training session that reduced to mere weeks what would normally take months or years to complete.

And then her mind turned to Arvin Sloane. He believed in her. He had said so himself, without a hint of condescension. She wouldn't have been sent on this mission if she couldn't do it.

If Arvin Sloane, the highest-ranking officer at SD-6, feels I can do this, then he must know some-

thing about me that I don't know, she thought. *I'll just have to believe him, and trust myself.*

And with that, her headache dissipated beneath her fingers. She opened her eyes in time to see the double doors to the theater swing open. The space beyond was dim, barely revealing the rows of seats that faced the main stage.

A woman stepped into the lobby. She was young, about Sydney's age, with long brown hair. Her left arm was in a cast and sling. She smiled at the group of girls, who had grown silent when the doors opened.

"Good morning, ladies!" she said cheerily in a British accent. "Thank you for coming down. We'll be starting in just a few moments. As I'm sure you already know, we have a single opening for a stage performer for Trevor Raven's *Age of Illusion* tour, which was temporarily postponed due to the injury of one of the performers."

She smiled and held out her plastered left arm as best she could. "I should know. I was there."

Everyone laughed pleasantly, including Sydney.

"My name is Angela Barker," she continued, "and until recently I was one of the performers in Mr. Raven's show. Unfortunately, I've been forced to take a hiatus from performing, but I am continuing to work on the show as an assistant to the stage manager, Mr. Viktor Romero."

As if on cue, there was movement from the darkened recesses of the theater, and then Romero himself stepped from the shadows into the lobby.

Sydney's smile vanished, a frown knitting her brow. Viktor stood with his hands clasped casually behind his back, a small smile on his lips. But Sydney looked at his eyes. There was no trace of joy there, only a coldness that flickered in his pupils.

Angela continued on. "Mr. Romero and I will be conducting the auditions, and once one of you has been chosen, my job will be to ease your transition to the performance team, with the hopes that we can continue the European part of the tour as quickly as possible."

Angela retrieved the sign-in sheet from the table and glanced over the list of names there.

"We will be calling you in one at a time. Have your head shot and resume ready."

She handed the sheet to Viktor, who looked over it without much interest as he disappeared back into the theater. Then she turned and entered as well, closing the doors behind her.

Sydney reached into her bag and pulled out the envelope of head shots, selecting two of the better ones that had been photographed and developed in the labs of SD-6.

As she looked over the pictures, she realized how few pictures she had at home. On her dresser back in the dorm room, she had a framed picture of Francie and herself. She had taken it during their first semester as freshmen, and every time she saw it, or even thought of it, it made her smile.

She had a small photo album as well, which sat on her bookshelf, a thin volume with more blank pages than she liked. The book contained family photographs. *But then,* she thought, *you have to have a family to have family photographs.*

There were no recent pictures in the book. There were no recent moments to capture. There were no Christmas photos because she hadn't celebrated the holiday with her father in years. There were no birthday photos because she couldn't remember the last time her father had celebrated her birthday with her, his arm around her shoulders, helping her blow out the candles and wishing her a happy birthday.

Sydney sighed, lamenting all the blank pages in her life, and zipped her bag shut, keeping the two pictures she had selected. She looked again at all the girls around her, wondering what the stories of their lives were.

She reached into the pocket of her jacket and pulled out a paperback of Chaucer. It was required reading for one of her sophomore English classes. With a sigh, she opened it to her bookmark and began to read, waiting for her name to be called.

* * *

"Nicole Bennet?"

Sydney looked up and raised her hand, quickly tucking her book back into her bag. Angela had been making regular appearances at the door every ten to fifteen minutes, and Sydney had been able to block the intervals out of her mind until she heard her name called.

Sydney followed Angela into the darkened theater and to a small table set up at the end of the aisle, just in front of the stage. There were two chairs: one in front of the table, for the applicant, and one behind the table, for Angela. Viktor would apparently not be sitting in on the interviews, at least not in sight.

Out of the corner of her eye, Sydney saw movement in one of the dark rows of seats toward the rear of the theater. She turned her head and saw two figures sitting deep in the shadows. Viktor, presumably, and one other person.

Sydney took a seat in the chair at the table and

for ten minutes answered Angela's questions about her experience, expertly inserting facts from the mental Rolodex she had constructed. This was apparently a preliminary weeding process, and Sydney hoped that she met the requirements to move on to the next round.

Angela's questions were pleasant but to the point, covering only subjects directly related to Sydney's ability to perform in the show. At the end, Angela thanked Sydney for coming and asked her to stay until after they had posted the list of candidates in the lobby.

Sydney rose from her seat and walked back up the aisle, stealing another glance into the darkness to see if the two figures were still there. Both seats were empty.

About a half hour later, Angela stepped into the lobby. All eyes were on her, the tension of waiting thick in the air.

"I'd like to thank everyone for coming. As you are well aware, we only have one position available for the show. You all showed great promise, but in order for us to expedite the selection process, we have narrowed our choices down to a select group. Failure to make the cut does not imply a lack of ability or talent on your part, but merely reflects the requirements we have."

She turned to a nearby wall, taped up a hand-written list, and turned back to face the girls.

"For those of you who have advanced to the second round, we will be starting shortly. Thank you."

She went back into the theater. As soon as she closed the door, the girls made a mad dash to read the list. Sydney hung back and waited. There was no need to rush up to the list. There were so many people clustered around it that it would be impossible to see.

A girl turned away from the list, shaking her head, and slung her bag over her shoulder. Sydney could see the tears forming in her eyes before the girl stepped out the door into the street.

Sydney felt a sudden tightness in her throat. *For me, this is all a lie,* she thought. *I'm just playing a part. Worst case, even if I don't make it, SD-6 will find another way to complete the mission. For these girls, it's their life. These jobs are how they live, how they eat. Am I taking that away from them?* she asked herself.

Six more girls left, backpacks hanging over slumped shoulders, and Sydney finally stood and walked over to the list. She waited until the girl in front of her had finished. After a moment the girl must have seen her name, because she barely swallowed an excited shout that escaped from her throat. She stepped away, leaving Sydney alone with the list.

She looked at the names written there. There were only about fifteen, half of those who had arrived with high hopes this morning. She looked down the list, and there, near the bottom, was her name.

I made it! she thought, relieved.

The door to the street opened again, and Sydney watched another girl leave, rejection evident in her shuffling walk. Sydney wondered again if she had robbed someone of her desperate need for employment, but then she remembered why she was there, remembered the shadowy figure in the darkness of the theater.

No, she thought. *Viktor did this. I am here because of something he is doing. SD-6 is involved because of the horrible things this man has done to other people, things he continues to do.*

Sydney *was* lying by being there, *was* lying by playing the part of Nicole Bennet, but Viktor was lying too. He was lying to the very people he worked for, using them to carry on his brutal business.

Sydney went back to her seat on the stairs. She looked at the handful of girls left, most of whom walked around the room in endless circles, their motors running high from their excitement.

But Sydney waited patiently, her hands folded in her lap, and thought of catching Viktor.

*   *   *

The second round of auditions was much longer, stretching late into the afternoon. Sydney's small breakfast had been hours ago, and she was glad she had thrown a granola bar from her flight into her bag. She ate it slowly, sharing half with another hungry girl sitting nearby.

One after another the girls went into the theater, returning some time later to retrieve her bag and leave, hoping she had gotten the job.

Finally, Angela stepped into the lobby and called, "Nicole." Sydney grabbed her bag and followed Angela once again into the theater.

As Sydney walked down the aisle, she noticed that the table and chairs were gone. The stage, which had been dark during the previous interview, was aglow under the intensity of the lights. Standing at the foot of the stage was Viktor, speaking to a man whose back was to Sydney. Sydney felt her left hand curl into a fist, and she forced herself to relax her fingers.

Angela stopped just before the stage and spoke to Viktor. As Sydney approached, Angela turned to her. "Nicole, I'd like you to meet Viktor Romero, the stage manager of the show."

Viktor stepped forward, all smiles, and held a hand out to Sydney.

"It's a pleasure to meet you, Nicole." Viktor said.

"It's a pleasure to meet you." Sydney replied, manufacturing a smile bright enough to conceal her disdain.

The man Viktor had been speaking with turned to face them, and Sydney froze. Viktor gestured to the man.

"Nicole, I'd like you to meet Trevor Raven."

Sydney blinked and stammered out a reply, extending a hand out to Trevor. She had never imagined he might actually be at the auditions, but here he was. Then she remembered the shadowy figure Viktor had been sitting with in the back of the theater; it must have been Raven. *Television doesn't do him justice.*

Trevor Raven was tall, with thick black hair and ice blue eyes that bore right into Sydney. He smiled warmly and shook her hand.

"Welcome, Nicole." Sydney recognized the Welsh accent at once. *I wonder how old he is . . . thirty?*

Angela stepped forward. "Nicole, what we're

looking for in this step of the audition process is stage technique and performance. We're going to run through some simple, standard routines."

"Of course," Sydney answered, hoping her voice was steady.

"If you just want to step up to the stage with Mr. Raven, we'll get started."

Sydney dropped her bag on the floor and stepped up to the narrow flight of stairs leading up to the stage. Trevor had already ascended, and turned to her.

Sydney took his hand.

6

SYDNEY'S HAND WAS STILL in Trevor's as they bowed. The applause was deafening, the sea of faces swelling as the crowd rose to their feet.

Behind her beautifully painted mask, one of the exquisite touches of her elaborate costume, Sydney's face was radiant with a smile as she gasped great, exhilarating breaths. She and Trevor stepped back as the rest of the assistants, all clad in equally beautiful masks and outfits, joined them. They formed a line across the stage, hands linked, and took a final bow as the red velvet curtain swung shut.

Back in the dressing room, the girls formed a

circle around Sydney, telling her what a wonderful job she had done in her debut performance.

"Nicole, you were wonderful!"

"Better than wonderful. *Amazing.*"

The door to the dressing room opened and Angela entered, wearing a headset. She gave Sydney a hug, her clipboard deftly tucked in her arm sling.

"Congratulations, Nicole," she said. "We're all so proud of you. Were you nervous?"

"Nervous? I was *terrified.*" Sydney replied.

Angela laughed. "Well, it didn't show. The performance went off without a hitch."

"Thanks to you," Sydney said. "I couldn't have done it without your support." She and Angela were roommates for the tour, and Angela had been great.

"Oh, don't mention it. Were you able to hear the cues all right?"

Sydney reached into her ear and extracted a tiny, delicate earpiece.

"Yes, perfectly. I never realized how important this would be."

Angela popped open her clipboard, revealing a section of foam cutouts layered between the boards. Sydney pressed her earpiece into the box labeled NICOLE.

"Everything in the show has to be precise,"

Angela said, collecting additional earpieces from the other assistants. "If anything is off by so much as a second, the illusion can be lost." She closed the clipboard, crossing off the names of those whose earpieces she had collected.

"Even now, after weeks of rehearsal, we still make adjustments. It's important that we be able to communicate with you guys during the show in case anything goes wrong."

Most of the girls had returned to their dressing stations, beginning the process of removing the makeup and costumes.

"Well, you better get changed." Angela hugged Sydney again, whispering in her ear. "You were great. We're so glad you're here." And then she was gone, off to do one of the million things she had to do before the next show.

Sydney went back to her dressing table. She stopped short, a gasp escaping her lips. There, on the table, was a beautiful bouquet of roses.

For a moment, Sydney had a wild thought that they were from Noah. But that was impossible. Who else?

There was an envelope tucked under the vase. With trembling fingers, she picked it up. NICOLE was written across the front in an elaborate, sweeping font. She opened the envelope and pulled out the card. Written neatly on its face in the same handwriting was:

Dear Nicole,

I cannot tell you how thrilled I am to have you with our troupe. I was hoping you would have dinner with me after the show. Please meet me at the Café de la Lune on Brighton. Hope to see you there.

—Trevor

* * *

Sydney crossed the dining room of the Café de la Lune , weaving between the tables. Tracking Viktor was her mission. Getting to know Trevor Raven might help her in that regard.

Or, it might just be a fun night with a famous (and cute) magician.

"Hello." Trevor said as he held her out her chair. She wore a short blue dress, and the skirt fanned over her legs as she sat down.

"Can I get you something to drink?" he asked as a waiter approached the table.

"What are you having?" she asked.

He gestured to his glass. "Just water with lemon."

She turned back to the waiter. "I'll have the same."

The waiter stepped away, leaving the two of them alone.

"Thank you for coming." Trevor said.

"Thanks for inviting me."

"I realized," Trevor began, unfolding his napkin and placing it on his lap, "that with all the rehearsals and preparations of the last few weeks, I haven't had the chance to sit down and talk with you. Angela's unfortunate accident threw things into a bit of a panic. As I'm sure you can imagine, a show like this is an incredible expense of time and money, and it's hard to explain to your investors why you may have to cost them more of both."

Sydney nodded, wondering what this was all about.

"So I wanted to take the time," he continued "now that the first show is over and we have a minute to breathe, to thank you for everything and tell you what an amazing job you've done."

"Thanks," Sydney said, pleased. She wished Noah were present to hear the compliment. Then she caught sight of Trevor's dimples and cool blue eyes. *Then again, I can do just fine by myself.*

"You're from Wales, right?" Sydney said after they had ordered.

"Yes, Swansea. Have you ever been there?"

"No, but I've heard it's beautiful. Is your family still there?" Sydney asked.

Slowly, he shook his head. "No. Unfortunately, I don't have any family. My parents died when I was very young, and I was an only child."

"I'm so sorry," Sydney said.

He sat back. "I was six when they died, and, not having any other family, I was sent to an orphanage. After two years I ran away and lived on the streets. I took up with a bad crowd. We were thieves, stealing a coin or two here, a loaf of bread there, anything we could to survive.

"One day, we came upon this old magician who was doing close-up magic on a street corner. I was sent to pick the man's pockets. I snuck up behind him while he was performing for a group of people and plucked the purse from his belt. Without even turning around he grabbed my hand. He was like a snake striking, he moved so fast. The rest of the gang went tearing off."

"What happened?" Sydney asked.

"Well, eventually the crowd left, and I knew I was in trouble. I thought he was going to take me to the police for sure. But when he turned back to me, he said that he could take me to the police or I could be his assistant.

He smiled wistfully, almost as if he had forgotten the story and was getting as much pleasure telling it as Sydney was hearing it.

"And that's how it started," he continued. "That was my first foray into magic. I traveled with him all over the world for years, learning all the tricks he could teach me, and seeing all the sights that I would have never seen, or probably even lived to see, had I stayed on the streets."

"What happened to him?" Sydney asked, curious.

"He passed away when I was in my teens." Trevor's eyes grew distant for a moment. "He opened an entire world for me."

They talked for another hour, enjoying an impassioned discussion about the merits of Fitzgerald and Hemingway and comparing their favorite works of Shakespeare. They talked about travel, with Sydney doing most of the listening as Trevor told her of the amazing places that his work had taken him. And then they shared a cab ride back to the hotel.

Before they said good night, Trevor took her hand in his and kissed it gently.

"Thank you for having dinner with me. I had a wonderful time."

"I did too." Sydney said, feeling flattered. It had never left her mind for a minute that this was a job—but it was hard not to be charmed by a man as worldly as Trevor Raven.

Trevor paused, and Sydney could see that he was debating asking her something. Finally he did.

"Would you mind if we did this again?" he asked.

"I'd love to," she blurted out before she could blink.

The elevator doors opened and Sydney stepped inside. She leaned back against the wall of the elevator, her heart fluttering. *Trevor is a lot older than you, and he's an assignment!* she scolded herself. *You're not in junior high!*

As quietly as she could, Sydney entered her suite, closing her bedroom door softly behind her before she turned on the light.

She hung her jacket on the back of the door and sat down on the edge of the bed as she unlaced her shoes. After she kicked them off, she lay back on the bed, staring up at the ceiling and listening to the tick of the clock on the bedside table.

The adrenaline that had carried her through the day had dissipated. The excitement of the show, and then the dinner with Trevor, had kept her going without a break. Now, in the silence and solitude, she was overwhelmed by exhaustion. She forced herself off the bed, staggered to her suitcase, and pulled out a pair of pajamas.

Once she had changed, Sydney flopped back onto the bed and turned off the lamp next to the clock, welcoming the darkness that swallowed her. In moments she fell fast asleep, but not before a single thought passed through her tired mind.

I wonder what happened in the housing lottery. Francie better have kicked some serious butt.

7

SYDNEY AWOKE THE NEXT morning to the rich smell of coffee. Sunlight spilled through the cracks in the blinds and painted the room with a warm glow.

She slowly sat up and rubbed sleep from her eyes, kicking her feet over the edge of the bed and resting them on the floor. She stretched, arms high overhead, reaching for the ceiling.

When she walked into the suite's common room, she saw what would become the standard breakfast on the tour: a rolling room-service table holding freshly baked croissants and muffins, a bowl of fruit salad, a pitcher of orange juice, and a steaming pot of coffee.

"Good morning."

Sydney turned and saw Angela sitting on the couch, a huge ledger balanced on her lap.

"Hi," Sydney replied, stifling a yawn.

Angela gestured toward the breakfast table. "Help yourself. I was up at the crack of dawn. I've already eaten."

"Thank you." Sydney said, and grabbed a small plate off the table. She picked a croissant and poured herself a cup of coffee, then sat down in the chair opposite Angela.

"Why were you up so early?" she asked.

"I wanted to finish these up before we left," Angela said, pointing to the ledger.

"What is it?"

"These are the cue logs from the shows. Each night we keep track of all the cues for the show, the ones we give you through your earpieces. It helps us determine which ones need to be worked on, whether to allow more time or to make a transition more quickly."

"How did we do last night?" Sydney asked as she picked the local newspaper off the table. She skimmed the front page—there had been a break-in at the National Gallery. *I wonder what was stolen?* she thought.

"Great. We need to make one or two minor adjustments, but overall it went well."

Angela looked up from the ledger, a mischievous gleam in her eye. "And speaking of last night, how did your dinner with Trevor go?"

Sydney stopped paging through the newspaper and looked up at Angela, who must have read the shocked look on Sydney's face because she laughed.

"Did you think we didn't see the roses at your changing table? That wasn't much of a secret, now was it?"

Angela's smile was warm and inviting. There was no malice in her question. Sydney smiled back, color rising in her cheeks.

"It went really well. It was nice after all the hectic weeks of prep to get a chance to sit down and talk with him."

"It's a custom of his," Angela said. "Whenever a new member is introduced to the crew, he takes them out to dinner. It makes you feel like family almost immediately."

Sydney nodded and took a sip of her coffee. She tried to convince herself that she wasn't a little disappointed that the dinner with Trevor was not a unique occurrence that she had been special enough to inspire.

"Time for a quick shower," Angela said, hopping to her feet. "We leave for Copenhagen in forty minutes."

* * *

The bus traveled to Dover and boarded a ferry that would take them across the English Channel.

Once aboard the ferry, the crew exited the bus and took the opportunity to stretch their legs before the long bus ride to Copenhagen. As the ferry crossed the channel, Sydney stood at one of the railings and stared out at the water. The air was thick with fog that rolled along the deck in soft waves.

Just before the ferry landed at Calais, everyone reboarded the bus, refreshed from the sea air. Sydney took her seat and stared out the window as the bus continued through Lille, Brussels, Amsterdam, and Hamburg, the sun slowly working its way down the sky.

She was lost in thoughts of home, staring aimlessly out the window, when she saw movement out of the corner of her eye. She turned and saw Trevor moving down the aisle toward the rear of the bus. As he passed by, his eyes fell on her, and he smiled. She smiled in return and watched him go by.

Sydney thought of all things they had in common that they had discussed over dinner. The one thing Sydney especially enjoyed about playing Nicole Bennet was the fact that she had many things in common with her alter ego, especially the love of literature.

I wonder if Noah likes Shakespeare? she wondered, looking out at the countryside.

Somehow Sydney dozed off because the next thing she knew she was awakened by a hand gently shaking her shoulder. She opened her eyes and turned to see Angela leaning over her.

"Hey," Angela whispered, "Sorry to wake you, but we're here."

Sydney looked out the window at the hotel that the bus had just pulled up to. She turned back to Angela.

"Wow. I must have been asleep for a while. I just wanted to close my eyes for a couple of minutes."

"It's the bus," Angela said. "I don't know why that is. I can't sleep on a plane to save my life, but the bus always knocks me out. Come on, let's get our stuff."

Sydney rose from her seat and joined Angela in line with everyone filing off the bus.

The evening air was cool, and Sydney caught her first glimpse of Copenhagen through tired eyes. Stifling a yawn, she grabbed her bag from the luggage compartment underneath the bus. She turned around and bumped directly into Trevor.

"Sorry!" she blurted out.

"It's all right." He smiled and slung his bag over his shoulder, tucking his hands into the pockets of his long black coat. "Did you sleep well?"

Sydney blushed. "I can't believe I dozed off."

"It was a long week for everyone." And with a smile he was gone, weaving among the throng of performers and crew huddled around the bus.

Sydney rubbed her hands together to warm them against the chill, and then stuck them into the pockets of her jacket. Her fingers brushed against something in her right pocket, and she pulled out a folded piece of paper.

She stepped away from the group, moving underneath a nearby streetlight, and opened the paper.

She recognized Trevor's handwriting immediately. Apparently he had not forgotten any of the pickpocketing tricks of his youth. He had been able to slip the note into her pocket without her noticing.

Nicole,

I was hoping I could see you tomorrow on our day off. I have something to show you. If you can, please meet me outside the main entrance of Copenhagen Central Station at 9:30 in the morning.

Please don't tell anyone. Things like this can make the show more complicated.

Trevor

* * *

Sydney carefully refolded the note and placed it back into her pocket. She was on a mission. Her priority was keeping tabs on Viktor. Getting involved with Trevor was professionally disastrous, as well as ethically questionable for any number of reasons.

The most important being Noah.

"Nicole?"

Sydney turned to see Angela approaching.

"Hey, there you are." Angela said. "I already checked us in. Do you want to go up?"

The girls walked through the revolving doors and through the lobby. As they rode up in the elevator, Sydney turned to Angela.

"It'll be nice to have a day off tomorrow, huh?"

Angela shook her head. "I wish I did."

"What do you mean?" Sydney asked.

"Well, the show's not on tomorrow, but the auditorium has to be prepped. Viktor and I will be there all day setting everything up with the local crew."

A thought stirred in Sydney's mind. If Angela was going to be with Viktor all day, then he couldn't be up to anything.

"All day?" she asked.

"All day." Angela sighed. "It's a shame too, because I was hoping to take a look around the city. Have you ever been to Copenhagen?"

"No."

"Well, then you should go sightseeing. As long as you have the opportunity, you should take it."

Sydney smiled and nodded. "Maybe I will."

8

THE NEXT MORNING SYDNEY stepped through the hotel doors and out into the streets of Copenhagen. The sun was cresting the roofs of the nearby buildings, and the sky was a glorious, cloudless blue.

She walked toward Copenhagen Central Station, passing a number of quaint stores that were opening up shop. Sydney paused for a moment to look in the window of an old bookstore, admiring the antique editions lined up neatly on a display shelf. The proprietor, an old man with a kind face and spectacles, waved to her as he dusted the counter near the register. Sydney waved back and then continued on, making a mental note of the shop's location in case she had an opportunity to go back and browse.

Sydney had a profound love for old books. Sitting on a shelf in her dorm, arranged carefully and meticulously cared for, was a large collection of antique books. It was a collection of all the great masters of literature, and while their value was undoubtedly very high, to Sydney they were beyond price. The books were her most prized and cherished possessions, for they had belonged to her mother.

The books offered Sydney a glimpse into her mother's heart and soul, demonstrating the passion she had for life, and for literature. She could imagine her mother holding them and turning the pages. As Sydney read them, she often wondered if her mother had felt the same exhilaration at reading the same passages Sydney did.

It surprised Sydney to think that each of the books had been a gift to her mother from her father. She could not imagine her father having a romantic bone in his body.

As Sydney crossed the street in front of the station, she felt a twinge of sadness regarding her mother, and tears welled in her eyes. As she wiped them away with her sleeve, Sydney hoped that wherever her mother was, she was proud of her.

Stepping up onto the sidewalk, Sydney was overwhelmed by the number of people coming in and out of the station. Wave after wave swept by her, businessmen and tourists alike all racing to make their train.

Sydney tried to pick Trevor out of the crowd, her eyes darting to each passing figure, but there were simply too many.

How am I supposed to find him here? she thought, moving forward with wary steps, dodging the people who blew by her in their hurry.

The sudden sound of laughter drew her attention to a small crowd that had gathered in the main plaza. Her curiosity piqued, she moved toward the group.

As she neared, a swell of cheers rose from the crowd, and their multitude momentarily parted to reveal Trevor standing in their midst, entertaining the crowd with sleight-of-hand tricks. Sydney stood at the edge of the crowd, smiling with awe as she watched Trevor dazzle the gathered throng with the most intimate of magical performances.

As his hands shuffled a deck of cards, his eyes flicked to her and he winked. He bent down and fanned the cards out toward a young boy in the crowd. The boy picked a card and Sydney was stunned to hear him address the boy in Swedish. The boy eagerly picked a card, and at Trevor's instruction he looked at it and placed it back in the deck, never showing it to the magician.

Trevor shuffled the deck again, the cards a blur in his hands. He then held the deck up for the entire crowd to see. He poised his right hand over the deck, the fingers rippling. Sydney looked at the crowd, struck by the wonder in their faces. During her performances with Trevor, the lights from the stage had made it almost impossible to see the faces of the crowd, and for the first time Sydney relished the opportunity to observe the reactions of those witnessing a performance by Trevor.

Trevor slowly raised his right hand, the fingers drawing together as if plucking at an invisible string. Sydney stared, suddenly slack-jawed and wide-eyed like the rest of the crowd, as a single card suddenly floated up from the middle of the deck, hovering in space between the deck and Trevor's hand.

Smiling, Trevor turned to the boy and asked him if that was his card. The boy, as stunned as ever, nodded slowly. With a laugh, Trevor relaxed his hand and the card dropped back down into the deck as the crowd exploded with applause. Sydney found herself clapping as well, as enthralled as the rest.

Trevor handed the deck to the boy as a souvenir, the child's eyes wide and excited, and waved to the crowd, thanking them for watching. The group splintered, and the people went on their way, talking excitedly about what they had just seen.

Sydney stepped forward through the dissipating crowd, and Trevor turned to her, a smile lighting up his face.

"You looked even happier here than you do onstage," Sydney said.

Trevor looked pensive for a moment, his fingers tracing the line of his jaw. His eyes searched the plaza as he considered a response.

"I love being on the stage," he said, turning to Sydney, "I do. But this . . ." He gestured to the narrow space around them, "This is where it really works." He suddenly stepped toward Sydney. "To be this close to people, without the lights and the props and the theatrics, and *amaze* them. That's what it's about."

"So what do we have planned for today?" she asked.

His eyes twinkled. "Let the magic begin."

He spun around and Sydney saw a small picnic basket a few feet away. Trevor picked it up and turned back to her, his eyes studying the pocket watch he had drawn from his coat. He snapped it closed and slid it back into his pocket, the silver chain gleaming in the sunlight. He looked back up and extended a hand to Sydney, his other arm holding the basket.

"Come on," he said. "We have a train to catch."

As confused as she was, curiosity and anticipation swelled in her, and Sydney placed her hand in his.

"Where are we going?" she asked.

"That's a surprise." He gently tugged at her hand, and the two of them ran for the entrance of the station.

They boarded the coastal train destined for Elsinore Station, sitting in a pair of seats that gave Sydney a breathtaking view of the waterway separating Denmark from Sweden.

As they neared Elsinore Station, Sydney turned to Trevor and tapped on the basket that rested on his lap.

"So what's in the basket?"

"Chicken sandwiches, fresh fruit, cheese, and bread, some bottled water, and chocolate truffles.

Oh, and I almost forgot." He opened the basket and pulled out a small package wrapped in brown paper. He handed it to Sydney.

"What's this?"

"Open it."

Sydney turned the package over in her hands, unwrapped the paper, and pulled out a small book bound in embossed leather. She gently opened the cover. The title, printed on delicate, smooth paper, read *Hamlet: Prince of Denmark*.

She closed the cover and let her fingers trace the grooves exquisitely carved into the leather. She turned to Trevor. "Thank you so much."

"You're very welcome. After our talk the other night at dinner, I thought it was something you would enjoy."

They stepped off the train at Elsinore Station, moving away from the edge of the platform as the train pulled away, the thrum of its engine sending vibrations through the boards beneath their feet.

They stood for a moment on the platform as the other passengers who had gotten off filed past them. After a moment, they were alone, and Sydney turned to Trevor.

"All right," she said with mock exasperation. "*Where* are we going?"

Silently, he pointed toward the horizon, and

Sydney followed the path of his hand with her eyes. Over the next hill stood a massive castle, its turrets reaching far into the sky.

"Kronborg Castle," he said, smiling at her amazed expression. "It was the castle made famous in—"

"Hamlet," Sydney interjected, *"Hamlet's castle."* She stared in utter disbelief, marveling at the building immortalized in one of Shakespeare's greatest works, stunned that she was seeing it with her own eyes.

"That's right." Trevor said. Sydney finally blinked and turned back to him, trying to find the words to express what she felt, but nothing came.

They took the short walk to the castle, the building looming ever larger as they approached. The sky was clear, with the sun warm on their faces, but a brisk wind blew, stirring the surrounding fields and the flags that graced the upper walls.

When they arrived at the castle, Sydney and Trevor passed through the beautiful Crownwork Gate, pausing briefly to view a stone tablet carved with a portrait of William Shakespeare before entering the courtyard.

They spent the morning taking a tour of the castle, admiring the Queen's Gallery and the Castle Chapel. They roamed the massive ballroom that covered the entire length of the castle's south wing. Sydney read aloud the details and history from a brochure she had picked up along the way as they examined the forty tapestries featuring one hundred Danish kings.

In the afternoon, they rested on one of the coastal batteries and ate lunch from the basket.

"Are you having a good time?" Trevor asked as he divided one of the sandwiches with a knife.

Sydney finished chewing a piece of apple as she nodded enthusiastically. *Hmmm, would I rather be here, at a castle, having a delicious lunch with a charming guy, or sitting in a stuffy lecture hall hearing my professor drone on about Chaucer? Tough choice.*

Trevor wrapped half of the sandwich in a napkin and handed it to Sydney.

"It's nice to have someone to share this experience with," he continued. "Someone who can really appreciate it. This would be lost on most people."

Sydney chewed her sandwich slowly, savoring both the food and the entire experience, sitting in a place of such history. She shook her head as she wiped her mouth with the napkin.

"I still can't get over it," she said. "I can't tell you how many times I've read *Hamlet*, how many times I've seen the play performed. It's unbelievable that I'm sitting in the very setting that inspired it."

Trevor reached for a bottle of water. "Well, believe me, I'm enjoying that you're enjoying it. It's nice to . . ." He paused, staring out at the horizon. He shrugged and looked back at Sydney.

"It's nice to have something in common with someone. The people in the show are my friends, my family, but at the same time we're all so different. The show is all we have in common. It's nice to be with someone who you have something in common with *outside* of the show."

A sudden gust of wind blew Sydney's hair across her face. She went to brush it away when she felt Trevor's hand across her cheek. He brushed her hair away from her eyes, tucking the errant strands behind her ear. Sydney blushed.

"Thank you," she said, resting her palm on her cheek to conceal the rising color of her skin.

"You're welcome," Trevor said. He started suddenly, snapping his fingers.

"I almost forgot," he said, reaching for the basket.

"What?" Sydney asked.

"The surprise," he answered.

"There's more than this?" Sydney asked, extending her arms to the beautiful countryside around them.

Trevor pulled a small cardboard tube out of the basket. He opened one end and turned it on its side.

A rolled-up sheet of paper fell into his hand. He dropped the tube back into the basket and unrolled the paper. His eyes flickered to Sydney.

"Come here," he said.

Sydney slid over so she was next to him, looking over his shoulder. He held a small poster, printed in rich, vibrant colors that sprang from the paper.

"It's just a proof," he said. "The finished ones will be much larger."

"What is it?" Sydney asked.

"It's a poster for the last part of the tour. We're unveiling a new illusion. 'The Dance with Death.'"

Sydney looked at the poster and felt a shiver run down her spine. At the top, written in bold red letters was TREVOR RAVEN. The artwork beneath was straight out of a horror film.

A number of dancers, presumably the show's stage assistants, were waltzing around a platform. Their dance partners were skeletons, tattered tuxedos of the grave hanging from their bones.

Trevor stood on the platform, a gleaming sword in each hand. He stood next to a massive glass coffin that stood on end. Locked within the coffin was another dancer, her arms folded across her chest in a posture of death. At the bottom of the poster, written in the same style used at the top was the inscription THE DANCE WITH DEATH.

"Um, wow," Sydney commented. "It's pretty grim."

"It's meant to be an homage to the show posters from the golden age of magic. Houdini, Kreskin, all of them used this macabre style. It was meant to use fear and dread to distance the audience from the idea of illusion and make them think of *magic*."

He rolled the poster back up and slid it into the tube.

"Why are you introducing the illusion so late in the tour?" Sydney asked.

"Well, we wanted to perform it earlier, but Angela's accident set it back. You see, she was the one who was supposed to be the girl in the box, and until we could get someone else in the show we couldn't do it."

"Who's going to do it now?"

He turned to her, squinting against the sunlight that washed across his face.

"Well, actually I was hoping you'd do it."

"Me?" Sydney squeaked. "Trevor, I can't. I just started on the show, and the other girls . . ." She was already where she needed to be to do her job.

She didn't need to take on more responsibilities as Nicole Bennet.

"Wait," he said, raising a placating hand to still her. "I understand your reservation about this. Yes, you are the newest girl in the show, and you're worried that it will seem as though I'm playing favorites and not being fair to the other girls who have been here longer, right?" He slid closer to her and placed a gentle hand on her arm.

"Okay, here's the thing," he said. "This is a big illusion, one that we've been prepping for the better part of a year, much longer than usual. Besides all the technical logistics of performing the illusion, there has been a considerable amount of choreography with all the girls. Everyone performs in this one, no one is left out.

"You have come along faster than any of us could have hoped for, but we don't have enough time to sufficiently run you through the routine to be one of the dancers. The only viable option is for you to be the featured girl in the illusion."

Sydney began to protest again, but he raised a finger to her lips, silencing her.

"Now wait, seriously, and listen. The featured girl is literally the simplest part. You get in the box and reappear moments later. That's one reason."

He dropped his hand from her lips and smiled.

"The second reason is that I *want* you to be the star."

His hand moved to hers, his fingers intertwining with hers.

"Nicole, I like you. I really do. Ever since we met I knew there was something special about you. And I know how hard it is to have something going on with someone you're working with."

Sydney blinked as the image of Noah flashed in her mind. She knew all too well what Trevor was saying. He cleared his throat and continued.

"I realize we haven't known each other very long, and I realize that that's an issue, but I just feel like I really know you."

She looked away, his words ringing in her ears. *Does he really know me?* she asked herself. What he knew about her was a lie, down to her very name.

They were sitting on the spacious grounds of Kronborg Castle because they had made a connection over dinner. They shared a love for literature, for art, for many things.

Why is this so complicated? she asked herself, her mind whirling, until he spoke again.

"Nicole?"

Because I am not who he thinks I am, she told herself. *And I am not who he thinks I am because I am on a mission, working to catch another person in his inner circle who is also lying to him.*

She wanted, at that very moment, to tell him the truth. Perhaps he could be trusted with the secret, could assist her in some way in catching Viktor.

But he could also get hurt. She was trained to do what she did. Trevor could no sooner work as a spy than she could attempt to perform the illusions he did.

"There's a lot going with the tour and every-thing, and I don't know what's going on in your head, but I just wanted to be up-front and honest with you," he finished.

"I know," she replied, the burden of his honesty only compounding her guilt.

"I just wanted to tell you how I felt," he said. "If I didn't, it was probably just going to come bursting out, probably in the middle of a performance, which might be embarrassing for everyone."

She laughed and he smiled, clearly relieved.

"I appreciate your telling me," she said. "But you're right, there is a lot going on with the show and everything, and I'm still trying to get adjusted, so . . ."

"I understand," he said, his delivery embarrassed

and quick, and she could see something die in his eyes. Maybe hope. "But you'll do the illusion?"

Sydney hesitated. She knew she should probably say no, but somehow, doing something kind for Trevor felt like the very least she could do. She nodded. "I'll do it."

He lifted her hand to his lips and kissed it. "Great." Then he reached into his coat and looked at his pocket watch once again. "What do you say we get back to the tour? There's so much more to see before we catch the train back to Copenhagen."

They spent the rest of the day exploring the castle and its environs, then caught a late-afternoon train back to Copenhagen, the sun setting low on the horizon, filling the train with coppery light. As they neared Copenhagen, dark storm clouds appeared overhead and it began to rain, bursts of lightning illuminating the train and peals of thunder shaking the windows.

Sydney watched as Trevor entertained a small group of passengers, in particular a small boy who didn't know that he had coins growing in his ears until Trevor showed him that handful of silver that he dropped into the boy's cupped hand.

Since working with the show, Sydney had become privy to how many of the great illusions worked. It had amazed her, and at the same time disappointed her, to see how many of them were done since it took some of the magic and mystery out of it.

But watching Trevor perform without the aid of smoke and mirrors mystified her. She could see none of the tricks, none of the distractions that were the key to many illusions. She was almost inclined to believe that there really was such a thing as magic.

When the train arrived in Copenhagen, the skies had opened up completely, and sheets of falling rain made the buildings just across the street impossible to see.

Trevor threw his coat over both their heads, and they ran out to the curb and hailed a taxi. Sydney slid over on the seat so he could get in, but he closed the door after her.

"What are you doing?" she asked, rolling down the window.

Trevor leaned in through the front window and handed the driver some money, telling the cab driver the name of the hotel, and then moved to Sydney's window.

"I don't think it would be a good idea for us to pull up together."

"But you're going to get soaked," Sydney protested.

"I'll be fine," Trevor said, droplets of rain coating his smiling face. "I'll catch another cab in a couple of minutes."

And then he was gone, disappearing into the downpour. Sydney sat back and rolled up the window as the cab pulled out into traffic.

A discarded newspaper lay on the seat from a previous fare. She picked up the paper and paged through it.

Suddenly she sat forward. She angled the paper toward the window so she could read by the light of the passing streetlamps.

ART THEFT BAFFLES POLICE

This can't be a coincidence, she thought as she quickly read the article. *Two robberies in the two cities that we've been performing in? This has to be Viktor's doing.*

When they arrived at the hotel, Sydney thanked the driver and exited the cab. As it pulled away, Sydney stood for a moment under the awning and watched the rain fall.

I'm not doing my job, she thought, guilt-stricken. *Instead, I'm traipsing around Hamlet's castle with Trevor Raven!*

Spy work was a lonely business, the tasks

performed in silence and, save the occasional partner, alone. A spy was meant to be unseen, unheard, unrewarded.

Sydney had gotten so caught up in the excitement of the show and all its trappings that she had neglected the reason she was here. And now Viktor was robbing galleries, and she had no information to give Sloane. At least, not yet.

Sydney turned and headed into the hotel, moving across the lobby toward the elevators. She would need to refocus and concentrate. Tomorrow, her primary responsibility would be to find out what Viktor was up to.

Any more sightseeing would have to wait.

9

THE NEXT DAY, SYDNEY stepped off the elevator into the lobby and took only a couple of steps before she saw Viktor. He was standing in the corner, talking to someone who was partially obscured by a pillar.

Sydney kept walking, blending into a group of tourists passing by, and ducked into the hotel gift shop. She absently began to thumb through a rack of postcards, stealing glances at Viktor every few seconds.

She still couldn't see who he was talking to very clearly. The man's face was turned to Viktor, who spoke urgently while he opened a flat package wrapped in brown paper. Viktor produced a small knife from his pocket and cut the twine that bound it. He peeled open the paper, but Sydney failed to see what it was. All she saw was Viktor nod, wrap the package back up, and hand it back to the man. Then they parted.

Sydney gasped. *It's the guard from the train!* The one she had knocked out in the hallway. Sydney waited until Viktor got in an elevator; then she exited the gift shop and headed for the doors in pursuit of the guard.

She followed at a safe distance, never allowing herself get too close to be discovered.

The guard walked through an open plaza, and Sydney slowed her pace. Out in the open, there would be no place for her to duck for cover should he suddenly turn around. She stopped in front of a newspaper stand and decided to wait for the guard to cross the expanse. Then she would hurry across to cut the distance between them.

The plaza was filled with pigeons that scuttled around, pecking for birdseed. Suddenly a little boy bolted through the flock, laughing and waving his arms. The pigeons rose into scattered flight, filling the air with the flicker of their beating wings, and Sydney lost her view of the guard.

She sprinted away from the newspaper stand and dashed to the street. The pigeons were returning to earth, and through them Sydney caught a glimpse of the guard ducking around a corner. She sprinted on, desperate not to lose him, and stopped only when she reached the corner. She peered around the building and saw the guard crossing the street to an outdoor café.

Sydney's view again was blocked, this time by a large fountain in front of the café. Tourists milled around the fountain, taking pictures and tossing coins into the splashing water.

She crossed the street, this time making sure the path was clear, and positioned herself among the tourists as she watched the guard enter the outdoor seating area of the café. He weaved his way through the dining patrons toward the door.

Moving slowly around the fountain, tossing a coin into the shallow bed, where it joined the countless other coins gleaming in the sunlight. From behind a bronze statue of a mermaid, Sydney watched the guard approach a table just inside the café door.

Sydney stopped short and ducked back out of sight. Seated at the table were the rest of the guards and Adrian Keller.

What are they doing here? Sydney thought. The guard leaned in to Keller and said something to him.

Keller immediately gestured to two of the guards, and they left the café, only to appear moments later driving a pair of black Mercedes sedans.

The remainder of the guards escorted Keller to the first car, a package tucked gently under his arm. As soon as his door was closed, the cars pulled away from the curb, their high-performance engines speeding them away.

Sydney debated catching a cab and following them, but thought she had a more important call to make. If Keller was working with Viktor, there would be another opportunity to follow them.

She stepped to the curb and hailed a cab. After it pulled up, she got in and gave an address to the driver as the cab glided back out into traffic.

Ten minutes later, the cab pulled to a stop in front of a small antique shop. Sydney paid the driver and stepped out of the cab, performing a cursory check to make sure she hadn't been followed.

As Sydney entered the store, a bell on the door chimed softly. She made her way toward the sales counter at the rear of the store. A pair of curtains hanging in a small doorway behind the counter parted, and an elderly man stepped through. He was cleaning a pair of wire-rimmed glasses with a red handkerchief, which he tucked into the breast pocket of his shirt. He hooked the glasses over his ears and smiled at Sydney.

"Can I help you?" he asked in his native Dutch.

"Yes," Sydney replied, her delivery and dialect flawless, "I was trying to find a gift for my grandfather."

"Did you have anything in mind?" the old man asked.

"I was looking for a watch," she said, giving him the code phrase.

He led her to a narrow flight of stairs that ascended to a small landing over the counter. A wooden gate blocked the stairs, with a small sign on it that read NO ADMITTANCE in Dutch. He lifted the latch and swung the gate open, gesturing for Sydney to go up. She climbed the stairs, the man following, and paused when she reached the landing.

The man moved past her to a closed door, pulling a set of keys out of his coat pocket. He slid one into the lock.

Sydney stepped through the doorway into a small attic room. Curtains were partially drawn over the single window, allowing a single shaft of light to cross the floor. The old man hit a switch on the wall, and the ceiling light came to life.

There were a number of cardboard boxes neatly lined up against one wall, and a couple of cracked vases in a corner.

In the middle of the room there was a table with a single chair. Both were very old. The laptop computer that sat on the table was not, its modern engineering sharply contrasting with the relics of another age that filled the building.

The man closed the door behind them and dropped the keys back into his pocket.

"Did you have any trouble finding us?" he asked in English, his accent evident in every syllable.

"Not at all," Sydney said.

"That's good," he said. He stepped to the computer and turned it on. The machine hummed to life. He turned back to Sydney.

"If you need anything, let me know."

"I will," Sydney said.

The old man stepped out the door and closed it behind him. Moments later Sydney could hear him descending the stairs. She turned to the computer and entered her access codes and passwords. After a moment she was logged onto the system, and her connection was rerouted again and again until the final connection was made.

There was a mini camera mounted on the top of the computer, and the red light came on. The screen flashed, and a moment later Arvin Sloane appeared on the display.

"Good morning, Sydney," he said.

"Sir."

"What news do you have for us?" he asked.

"I saw Adrian Keller this morning."

"Where?"

"At a café here in Copenhagen. Earlier today, Viktor met with one of the guards from the train mission in Japan. The guard had brought some kind of package to him. Viktor looked at it and then gave it back to the guard, who I tailed to the café."

Sloane looked grave, rubbing at the short growth of beard that shadowed his face.

"After Japan, Keller went underground. We were wondering when he would resurface. Did you see what the package was?"

"No," Sydney replied, "but I have an idea."

"What's that?" Sloane asked.

"There have been robberies in every city we have visited."

"What kind of robberies?"

"Art galleries. When I read the first story I didn't make a connection, but after the second one I began to suspect something was going on."

"Art theft certainly would be Keller's specialty," Sloane said.

"I'm not sure I understand what Viktor's involvement would be in stealing art."

"Well, stolen works of art can fetch a fortune on the black market. Viktor could be using the profits to purchase weapons. The whole idea of his using the tour as cover is exactly what we anticipated. We'll look into the thefts on our end and see if we can get any more information. What's next on the schedule?"

"Tonight we have a show, and then tomorrow morning we move on to Amsterdam."

"That's fine," Sloane said. "Check in with us in there and we should have more information for you."

"All right," Sydney said. She was reaching for the keyboard to log off the system when Sloane spoke again.

"Sydney?"

Her hand paused over the keys, her eyes meeting Sloane's on the display.

"Sir?" she asked. Her hands suddenly felt cold. *This is where he tells me that he thought I would have more progress to report,* she thought, *because although he may not say it out loud, he's thinking he should have sent someone else.*

But Sloane simply smiled. "Excellent work. Didn't I tell you that you could do this?"

And just like that, the rising panic that had been

building in her suddenly dissipated. *How does he do that?* she thought. *How, with a few simple words, a kind gesture, does he make me feel better?*

But the questions in her mind were harshly answered by a thought that drove a spike through her. *Maybe it's just because no one's ever done it before. People who care do things like that.*

No one had ever cared.

10

AS SYDNEY STEPPED OUT into the footlights in Amsterdam, she couldn't take her eyes off a massive ebony case that occupied the center of the stage. It stood on one end like a midnight monolith, casting a dark shadow.

Trevor stood alongside it, running his hand along the smooth finish. "What do you think?" he asked.

"It's actually kind of scary-looking," Sydney replied. It looked eerily like a coffin.

Trevor laughed. "Exactly the reaction I was

hoping for. There's nothing to be worried about. Come on, I'll show you."

He led her across the stage to the box and opened the front. The inside was pitch black. Trevor stepped inside the case and tapped on all the surfaces with his knuckles.

"See, solid. Or is it?" He stepped out of the case and kneeled down, tapping the bottom panel.

"The inside of the box is basically an elevator. You get inside, we close the door, and the interior section drops down below the stage at the exact point where the floor opens to the basement."

"What are these?" she asked, pointing to a series of slits cut into the sides of the case.

"That's where the swords go," Trevor replied.

"The *what*?" Sydney asked.

"Don't worry!" Trevor laughed. "You'll be down and out of harm's way long before that happens. Then you come up through the elevator and you're suddenly back onstage. But to the audience, you never left, and you magically survived."

The rest of the girls were starting to assemble on stage. The house lights went down, and red stage lights illuminated the space. Angela crossed the stage to Sydney and Trevor.

"We're ready for a run-through," Angela said.

"Great," Trevor replied. "Let's go through it once without Nicole, so she can watch from up here to see what happens."

He stepped offstage into the wings. Angela moved next to Sydney. "Nervous?" she asked.

"A little," Sydney said. And despite everything she'd been through the past year, she actually was. "Yeah, I am," Sydney said, managing a nervous smile. Angela patted her arm.

"You'll be fine, trust me. Once you see how it's done, it moves like clockwork, just like the rest of the show. You'll feel like you've done it a million times."

The speakers overhead popped slightly, and then music began to emanate from them. The tune was dark, mysterious. Trevor's voice suddenly boomed from the speakers.

"Tonight you will witness one of the great marvels of ancient magic. A forbidden spectacle of the ages. The Dance with Death!"

"Is he doing that live?" Sydney asked.

"No," Angela said, "it's recorded. This is where he makes a costume change, and the recording gives him the opportunity to change offstage while keeping the audience interested in the act."

The girls emerged onto the stage. They each danced with a papier-mâché skeleton that wore the ragged tuxedo the poster promised. They waltzed across the stage in time with the music, their movements fluid from endless hours of practice.

Trevor was right, Sydney thought. *There's no way I could have learned all this before the show.*

Two of the girls, Beth and Brianne, walked onto the stage, leading an invisible third.

"That'll be you," Angela whispered.

Beth and Brianne mimed tying her at the wrists.

"Then they'll tie your hands," Angela said.

Overhead, the narration continued.

"Our lives balance on the precipice of life and death, of dark and light, the two halves joined in an eternal dance in which death is the victor."

Beth and Brianne then walked to the box, opened the doors, and ushered the imaginary Sydney inside, closing the doors behind her.

"But there are those who defy death."

Trevor walked onstage, carrying a magician's wand about three feet long. He opened the box and rapped on all the outside surfaces with the wand, showing the audience that it was solid. Trevor then slid the wand through a pair of slots along the frame, barring the door.

"Okay," Angela said, "now the elevator drops, and you're in the basement. You don't even have to get off the elevator—in fact, you shouldn't because it comes right back up only a minute later."

Trevor pushed the box, and it spun, the base fitted with wheels.

"See, the box is now free of the elevator, so it can move around. That way the audience doesn't think there's an escape through the floor."

The box slowly spun around the stage. Beth and Brianne had acquired macabre dance partners of their own, and they whirled about the coffin.

The narration continued, but Sydney, drawn by the action, heard none of it. All of the assistants suddenly thrust their hands into the mouths of the skeletons and pulled out gleaming swords. The skeletons collapsed to the stage, useless piles of cloth and bone.

And yet the dance continued, the music building. The girls whirled and whirled, their movements a blur, accented by the flashes of light reflected off the swords.

Suddenly, they leaped forward and one by one thrust the swords into the spinning box. Sydney jumped as the blades passed through the box, their razor tips protruding out the opposite side. Beth handed her sword to Trevor, and he thrust it through the front, straight through the heart, stopping the coffin.

Then he pushed it again, back in the direction it had come. The box spun the opposite way, and as it passed each girl pulled her sword from it. Finally it neared the spot where it had started and Sydney understood.

"So it gets back there, and the elevator pops back up."

"Exactly," Angela said. "The last sword comes out, the elevator comes up, and there you are."

The box stopped and Trevor pulled the sword out. He slid the bar from the doors and opened them. The music rose in an explosion of chords and then stopped.

He turned to Sydney and Angela, smiling.

"What do you think?" he asked Sydney. "Ready to give it a try?"

The cast ran through it twice, the first time at half speed. They tied her wrists and put her in the box, and Sydney was only momentarily claustrophobic before the elevator dropped. It stopped in the dimly lit basement, and Sydney waited patiently on the platform.

She could hear everything going on above her, and after a minute, she made sure her hands and feet were clear as the elevator lifted her back into the dark confines of the box. A second later the doors opened and she stepped out onto the stage.

They ran through it a second time and then broke for lunch, everyone selecting hungrily from the table of sandwiches and salads. Everyone sat casually around the floor of the stage, and Sydney listened intently as everyone laughed and told stories of past tours and illusions.

After lunch, Trevor decided on a full runthrough.

"Let's do the works on this one," he said. "Lighting, effects, everything. And let's run earpieces, I want to start nailing the final times down."

Angela handed out earpieces to everyone, and everyone went off to change into costumes. Sydney emerged from the dressing room in a blue sequined gown with a matching mask. The other assistants wore similar dresses of different colors with masks of the same shade.

Sydney stood behind the curtain and looked out at the stage. Somewhere behind the back curtain, a fog machine was producing billowing clouds that swept across the stage floor and out into the first two rows of the audience. The ebony coffin appeared to hover in the mist.

Angela walked up, clipboard in hand.

"Are you ready?" she asked.

Sydney nodded. Beth and Brianne appeared by her side. Beth held the loop of rope.

"Let me show this to you," she said.

The loop of rope was a common magician's trick. Beth tied it, and to the ordinary eye it seemed like a tight bind, but in reality it fell apart with a simple twist of the wrist.

The music began, and Sydney watched the rest of the girls float across the stage, the fog swirling about their feet. The narration started, and Sydney looked over her shoulder. Trevor stood a few feet behind her, dressed in a flowing black cape with red satin lining. He looked at her and winked. Sydney smiled and looked back at the dancers.

A moment later Beth and Brianne ushered her onto the stage. They tied her hands and led her into the box, closing the door behind her. Red light filtered in through the narrow cuts in the box, and Sydney could see the fog covering her feet.

Raven made his way onto the stage, and the fog almost seemed to part before him. When he slid the wand across the doors, the elevator dropped to the basement.

Sydney looked up and watched the floor close with a hidden door. She twisted her wrists and the rope slid off into her hands.

"All right, Nicole," Angela's voice said in her ear. "Sixty seconds."

Sydney stepped off the platform for a moment

and stretched her arms. She saw a sudden flash of blue light out of the corner of her eye. She turned and saw the light spilling through a crack in a door across the room. Then she heard Viktor's voice.

Slowly, she crept across the room, moving as silently as she could toward the door, hoping that a loose floorboard wouldn't give her away.

Sydney jumped when Angela spoke again.

"Thirty seconds."

Sydney looked through the crack in the door, holding her breath.

Viktor stood on the other side of the door in a small room. Keller was with him. Both of them were looking intently at something, its surface bathed in the blue light. She wanted to stay and figure out what they were doing, but Angela spoke again.

"Fifteen seconds."

Sydney stepped back from the door and bumped into a crate. She saw Viktor and Keller look up. She ran back as quietly as she could. She risked a look over her shoulder and saw a shadow move across the light on the door. Someone was coming.

She leaped onto the platform. Her feet no sooner made contact than it began to rise out of view.

The doors sprang open and she stepped out,

breathing heavily. The music came to a halt, and Trevor turned to her.

"Are you okay?" he asked.

"Yes," Sydney said between breaths. "It's just very exciting."

Trevor smiled at her.

"Yeah, I guess it is," he agreed.

THE NEXT MORNING SYDNEY went for a walk. The sky was gray and cloudy, and by the time she had walked two blocks, rain began to fall. She opened the umbrella she had brought along, and disappeared among the dozens of umbrellas dotting the street.

She walked for about twenty minutes, retracing and altering her route again and again to make sure she wasn't being followed, finally stopping at an old bookstore.

Sydney ducked out of the rain, stepping through the archway of the bookstore as she lowered her umbrella. She snapped it shut and shook the droplets onto the sidewalk so she wouldn't track the rain through the store.

She wiped her shoes on the mat and crossed the floor, nodding to the old woman at the counter, who nodded in return.

"Hello," Sydney said. "Do you speak English?"

The woman nodded, and Sydney continued.

"I was wondering if you had any first editions of Chekhov?"

"In English?" the woman asked.

"No," Sydney replied, "Lithuanian."

"Let me check," the woman said. "Take a look around, and I'll let you know."

There were a couple of customers roaming the aisles. Sydney joined them momentarily, thumbing through vintage leather-bound editions of Dickens and Keats.

When the customers had rounded a corner to another aisle, the old woman appeared and gestured to Sydney. She silently followed the woman through a velvet curtain leading to a back storage room.

There was a door on the other side of the room, and Sydney could see stairs. The woman left her alone, and Sydney went down the stone steps into the darkness. There was a single light on in the cellar. It swung back and forth on a heavily taped cord, its sweeping motion stretching and shortening the shadows.

Sydney stepped off the stairs and on to the floor, unbuttoning her wet jacket as she went, and froze.

Noah.

He sat in front of a computer, his brown hair rumpled and dark circles under his eyes. He rose and stepped toward her with his hands thrust deep into the pockets of his black jacket.

"Hi."

Sydney stared at him with disbelief, the fingers of her left hand still fixed on the buttons of her jacket, the fingers of her right white-knuckling the handle of the umbrella.

"Noah!" she cried, suddenly dropping the umbrella and running to him. She flung her arms around him, memories of Santa Barbara flooding her brain. "What are you doing here?"

He hugged her back hard, his skin smelling of coffee and Ivory soap. "I got back from my mission early, and Sloane sent me in to assist you. He said there was some information that they've acquired, and he thinks it's become a two-person job."

Stepping back to drink him in, Sydney finished undoing the buttons of her coat, slid it off, and hung it on a hook jutting from one of the ceiling beams.

"I don't have all the details," Noah continued.

"Sloane said he would fill us both in when we were here." He turned and gestured to the computer, the screen emanating a soft glow. "Let's find out."

Wishing they could be anywhere but in front of an SD-6-linked computer, Sydney sat down in the chair Noah offered.

"After ten hours in an economy window seat, I'm glad to stand," he said, running his fingers along her cheek.

He kneeled down beside her as she fired up the monitor, her heart pounding wildly.

The computer beeped, and the red light on the camera lit up. Noah tuned to face the screen, his hands by his side and his posture going rigid. Sydney realized there wasn't going to be anything else exchanged between them. She sighed softly and turned to the computer as well.

The screen lit up, and Sloane appeared in the display.

"Agents Bristow and Hicks, thank you for joining us on such short notice. Agent Hicks, I trust your flight went well?"

"It went fine, sir."

"Good. Now, Agent Bristow, I know that Agent Hicks's sudden appearance on your mission is undoubtedly surprising, but I assure you that I have answers forthcoming."

He was suddenly joined by an attractive woman with jet-black hair wearing a dark, well-cut pantsuit.

"Agents Bristow and Hicks, let me introduce you to Agent Carlino of our research division. The gallery robberies may be the key to this entire mission, as Agent Carlino will explain."

Carlino took this as her cue from Sloane, and she addressed Sydney and Noah.

"We have concluded that there is a link between the art thefts, and that Viktor Romero is orchestrating them. However, our original assumption that he wanted to sell them for profit is incorrect."

"Why?" Sydney asked.

"The paintings themselves are not considered to be extraordinarily valuable." Carlino hit a key, and the bottom half of the monitor was suddenly occupied by photographs of five stolen paintings.

"They are works of lesser-known artists throughout the centuries, none of whom has been of particularly high regard."

"Then why steal them?" Noah asked.

"That was our question," Sloane said. "Why go to all that trouble to steal these pieces, and walk right past the Degas and the Rembrandts."

"And there seemed to be no connection, no pattern between the pieces," Carlino added. "They are works of different artists, in different artistic styles, and in different centuries."

"Then what is the connection?" Sydney blurted out, confused. Noah cocked an eyebrow at her. Sydney bit her lip and brushed a strand of hair behind her ear.

"I'm sorry, I don't mean to be so candid, but I can't do my job if I don't know what I'm looking for."

"You're absolutely right Sydney, I apologize," Sloane said. "It is not our intention to string you along or impair your ability to complete your mission, but this is new information for all of us, and we're still trying to get a grip on it. Agent Carlino, please continue."

Carlino cleared her throat.

"These are the five paintings that were stolen. The images here are direct from the archive offices of the museums that housed the paintings."

Carlino hit another switch and one of the paintings, a beautiful landscape, filled the entire bottom half of the screen.

"One of the techniques that museums use to determine the authenticity of the paintings they have is ultraviolet scanning. This technique reveals the base layers beneath the final work."

The painting on the screen suddenly changed,

its image rendered almost black and white, revealing a bizarre series of lines and images.

"What is this we're looking at?" Noah asked.

"This is the scan of the painting you were just looking at," Carlino said. "This too was acquired through the museum's archives."

Sloane cleared his throat and spoke.

"Many of the great painting masters, while now revered for their work, did not experience a climate of success while they were working. The materials they needed were often expensive, so it was not uncommon for an artist to reuse a canvas."

"Sometimes it's a rough sketch of the final painting," Carlino added, "sometimes it's an entirely different work."

"But not in this case, right?" Sydney asked.

Sloane smiled and nodded.

"Correct, Sydney."

The image of the painting shrank to its original size and position beside the others. Each of the other paintings had changed to that strange monochromatic hue, revealing the hidden lines beneath. Sloane continued.

"Now, again, you have to keep in mind that each of these paintings comes from a different museum. They are works of different artists in different styles, so there would have been no reason for anyone to make a connection between them. But we did."

The paintings on the screen suddenly floated up, crisscrossing one another and fitting into one large square, with a small section in the middle missing.

"Oh, my God," Sydney said.

Put together, the paintings revealed a massive diagram of mysterious marks and images. At the center was a circle filled with words in what Sydney immediately recognized as Latin. The borders of the diagram were illustrated with pictures of a country village.

"What are we looking at?" Noah asked.

"It's called a Hermetic Citadel, the great seal of an ancient magical order. The Order of Calistrano." Sloane said.

There was a long pause, and then Noah, with an incredulous shake of his head asked, "And who would that be?"

"Vincenzo Calistrano was a sixteenth-century magician," Carlino said. "Fleeing religious persecution, he disappeared and formed an underground society in his name."

"How does this figure into the mission?" Sydney asked.

"At the height of his popularity, before he disappeared from public life, magic was the power of the day." Sloane said. "It was a time before the real birth of the modern sciences, and as a result, magic was the science of the unknown, the key which would unlock the mysteries of the universe. Calistrano was believed to have discovered the ultimate key. A source of power that, in his own words, 'would rival that of God.'"

"That couldn't have been a popular thing to say," Noah said.

"It certainly was not, particularly with the Vatican. After a failed assassination attempt on their part, Calistrano disappeared and formed his underground society, composed mainly of—"

"Artists," Sydney finished.

Sloane smiled and nodded. "Right."

"What about the source of power he discovered?" Sydney asked.

"That is a secret that he took with him to the grave," Sloane said. "We also discovered that this seal, besides being the mark of Calistrano's order, is also a map."

"A map of what?" Noah asked.

"The crypt of Calistrano," Sloane said.

There was a moment of heavy silence in the

room as the information washed over Sydney and Noah. Carlino finally spoke.

"When we studied this diagram, we discovered that it was drawn by Calistrano himself. If you look closely, you can see his signature in the lower right-hand corner. The theory is that he drew the picture and then divided it into pieces that were painted onto black canvases. He was the only one who ever saw the entire picture. The canvases were passed down through the generations to different members of the society, who made their own artistic impression on them. No one ever knew who made the previous paintings or where they went."

"Then how were they supposed to find the crypt?" Noah asked. "A map divided for centuries, and the secrets kept from even the members of the society. Why?"

Sloane leaned forward, his face looming larger on the screen. "Calistrano believed very deeply in the path of fate. He believed that a single 'chosen one' would discover the secret and, having done so, would earn the victory of the power he discovered."

"And Viktor has discovered it," Sydney added.

"Yes." Sloane said. "It explains his role in Trevor's show."

"How?" Noah asked.

"Trevor has what is considered to be the greatest library of magic in the world. He has volumes that date back centuries, and he has spared no expense in building his archive."

"I read about that," Sydney said. "He plans to eventually build a museum for the public."

"That's right. But for now, Viktor has been using the library to supplement his search."

Sydney frowned, her eyes growing dark. "He's been stealing information right under Trevor's nose."

"Presumably," Sloane said.

"How did you guys discover all this?" Noah asked.

Carlino smiled. "Our resources are rather formidable as well."

"So do we know where the crypt is?" Noah asked.

"No," Sloane replied. "At least, not yet. If you notice, the picture is still missing one painting to complete it.

"Most likely they think that the secret to the crypt is hidden in the details of the painting rather than under the painting."

"No," Sydney said. "They know."

"How do you know for sure?" Sloane asked.

"Yesterday, during rehearsal, I was in the basement of the theater for one of the illusions, and I saw Viktor and Keller. I couldn't see exactly what they were doing, but I only noticed what was going on because of this purple light I saw."

"Ultraviolet," Carlino said.

"So they do know," Sloane said. He rubbed the stubble on his chin. "That's fine, we just need to beat them to the next painting."

"How does the key fit into this?" Sydney asked.

"Our best guess is that whatever is in the crypt can only be opened with the key."

"But if they knew that they needed the key, then why are they still pursuing the location of the crypt?"

"I don't know. They may have another way of opening the crypt, but we don't know what that is."

"So what's our plan?" Noah asked.

"The last painting is on display at the Rijksmuseum there in Amsterdam," Sloane said.

He hit a button, and a picture appeared on the screen, with the name of the artist beneath it. Sydney and Noah instinctively leaned forward, committing it to memory.

"We have floor plans and tech equipment en

route to you. Tonight you will break into the museum and get the painting. When you get back, you will scan it using a handheld scanner that we have specially modified for the mission. We'll analyze the data, and from there we should be able to locate the crypt."

THAT EVENING, A TELEPHONE repair van

stopped just down the street from the Rijksmuseum. The driver's door opened and a technician
got out, strolling casually to the rear of the van.
He opened the back door and pulled out orange
safety cones and traffic horses, using them to block
off the rear of the van and direct traffic around it.

He grabbed a crowbar out of the back and lifted
the cover off a manhole a couple of feet from the
van. The technician pulled a flashlight out of his
tool belt and peered down the manhole. He clicked
the flashlight off and headed back to the driver's

seat. Then he got in and closed the door behind him, taking his construction helmet off.

"We're good," Noah said, resting the helmet on his lap. Sydney sat in the passenger seat, her hair tucked up under her own helmet. She stared at a series of schematics and blueprints, and she flipped nervously from page to page.

"Sydney," Noah said, "are you all right?"

She turned to him, peering out from under the brim of the helmet.

"Yeah, I just . . ."

She flipped aimlessly through the pages again, then slid them back into a binder.

"I still haven't quite gotten the hang of using blueprints as a reference," she said. "It's hard for me to look at these things and see a *picture* of where I'm supposed to go. Even with all this, I feel like I'm going in blind."

She stared out the window, frustrated. She hated admitting a weakness to Noah.

"Hey," he said softly.

She turned back to him, and he reached over the seat of the van, grabbing the laptop off the backseat.

"Let me show you something."

He turned on the computer and hooked an Internet cable to it that ran to an antenna on the roof.

"What's different about this place?" he asked. "What makes it different from almost every other target that we drop into?"

Sydney shrugged and shook her head.

"I don't know," she said.

"It's open to the public," Noah continued. "It's a museum. It's not a missile silo, or a weapons manufacturing plant. People are supposed to want to come here, to know everything about it."

He typed, entering something into a search engine.

"Now let's say you want to go on vacation someplace. What do you do before you go? You research it, right? You try and find out as much as you can, so when you get there, you know where you want to go and what you want to see. And what's the best way of doing that?"

"The Internet," Sydney replied.

"That's right," Noah said. "Now let's say you wanted to visit Amsterdam, and you're an art fan, and you figure while you're in town you should check out a museum or two. In fact, the Rijksmuseum sounds like the place to go. So what do you do? You look it up on the Internet."

He turned the laptop toward her, and there on the screen was the home page for the Rijksmuseum. He pointed to various icons on the screen.

"Here you can read the history of the museum. Click on this and you can see what the additions to the gallery are, and over here . . ."

He rolled the muse over to an icon and clicked, bringing up a page of pictures. Sydney leaned forward.

"This is where you can take a virtual tour of the museum," Noah said. "It has pictures of every level, every exhibit, including room forty-seven of the basement and Philips Wing, exactly where you're going."

He clicked on a picture, and he was able to actually pan around with the mouse.

"Here's your access panel, there's the security camera, and there's your back exit, past the statue and up the stairs."

He handed the laptop over to her.

"Take a look at this, see if it helps. Blueprints give us access and security protocols, but you're right, if we can't see what color the walls are and what the furnishings look like, we do go in a little blind."

He put his helmet back on.

"I'm going to go start the security taps. When you're done, bring the laptop and meet me down in the tunnel."

He got out of the van. Sydney watched him in

the side mirror as he walked along the the van and disappeared down the manhole.

She looked at her watch. Time was running short. She scrolled through the pictures for a couple of minutes, introducing herself to the areas she would be entering. When she was done, she logged the computer off the Internet and closed the lid. She exited the van and, carrying the computer under one arm, went down the manhole.

Noah was splicing wires into a main security box.

"You good?" he asked.

"Yes," Sydney said. He took the computer from her and patched the splices into a connector on the back.

"Thanks," Sydney said.

He looked up and gave her a smile that made her feel woozy. "You're welcome."

The screen lit up, and Sydney saw it was hooked in to the security system.

"All right," Noah said, "we're in. When I pop the system, they'll be calling the security company for backup. I've routed the phone line to here, so I'll take the call and stall them. The only trouble on your end will be the guards. On the night shift, there shouldn't be too many, so just avoid contact if you can. Do you have everything?"

"Yes," Sydney said.

She took off the helmet, her hair spilling out, and unzipped the front of the orange jumpsuit. She peeled it off, revealing black combat fatigues underneath.

Noah pointed down the tunnel.

"Twenty yards up is your access panel. Past that and you're in the basement, and you know where to go from there. You got your ears on?"

Sydney slid a radio headset out of her tactical bag and slid it over her head. She turned away from Noah.

"Walkie check" she whispered into the headset.

"Good check," Noah said, tapping his earpiece.

Sydney slid a black mask over her head, and she was practically invisible in the darkness. She headed down the tunnel.

"Hey," Noah said.

She stopped and turned.

"Good luck," Noah said, and immediately went back to work.

Sydney nodded. She loved her job—but she would have preferred to spend one-on-one time with Noah outside of work.

* * *

Sydney quietly slid aside an acoustic ceiling tile and peered into the space below. The gallery was empty. She tied a rope to a water pipe, let the end fall to the floor, and slid down the rope.

"I'm in," she whispered into the headset.

"Copy," Noah replied. "Security system is in complete shutdown, screens are blank on their end. They just made the call, and I stalled them, so we've got a couple of minutes to work with."

"Any guards to worry about?" Sydney asked.

"Negative. Once the alarm went down, they all scurried to the security station on the main floor. Do your thing."

Sydney crept along the hallway, using her memories of the blueprints and Web site to guide her. She saw a sign pointing to room 47, and she continued.

Room 47 was wall-to-wall paintings, the frames mere inches from one another, with a tiny description card posted beneath each.

"Noah," Sydney whispered, "there's about a thousand paintings in here."

"Well, if that wasn't bad enough," Noah said, "you're going to have company in about a minute. A guard is heading down there right now."

"What?" Sydney gasped.

"Relax," Noah said. "I'll talk you through. Look over your shoulder. See the camera?"

Sydney looked behind her and saw a security camera on the ceiling.

"Yeah, there you are," Noah said. "I've got eyes on the whole place. It's like a maze down there. Do as I tell you and you'll stay out of sight. Just move where and when I tell you to move."

At the other end of the wing, Sydney heard a door open and swing closed.

"All right," Noah said, "the game's in play. Move to your left and hide behind that wall."

Sydney moved, stealing behind the corner and close to the wall. She heard approaching footsteps and saw the spill of a flashlight beam across the opposite wall.

"Okay, get ready," Noah said. "When I say, duck back out the way you came and go straight down the corridor."

The flashlight beam grew closer, the circle of night narrowing on the wall. Suddenly it veered off as the guard turned a corner.

"Now," Noah said, "go!"

Sydney went, moving stealthily down the corridor. At Noah's direction she turned to her right into an alcove.

"All right, hold there for a second."

Sydney took a deep breath, letting it out as

slowly and quietly as possible. She scanned the walls around her, trying to get her bearings.

Where is the access panel from here? she thought. *Where do I*—

She stopped suddenly, her eyes falling on a painting. She tiptoed forward, moving closer. The painting was about one foot square, dwarfed by the larger works on the wall. She read the tag beneath it.

"Noah," she whispered, "I found it. I've got the painting."

"Grab it, and wait for me to make sure you're clear of the guard."

Sydney reached up and took the painting off the wall, being careful not to bump it against the others ones and alert the guard. She gently placed it on the floor and unzipped her bag. She was reaching for the soft case to hold the painting when her hand bumped into the portable scanner. She paused, then grabbed the scanner.

"Okay, Sydney," Noah said, "get ready to move."

"I'm not ready," Sydney whispered.

"What?"

The scanner hummed to life in Sydney's hand, and she rolled it across the surface of the painting, covering every inch of the canvas.

"Sydney, what are you doing?" Noah asked.

"Just give me a second."

She dropped the scanner back in the bag and slid the cover over the painting, slipping the bag back over her shoulder.

"Okay, Noah," Sydney said, taking a breath, "I'm ready."

"Happy to hear it, just waiting on you," Noah said, and Sydney could tell he was annoyed. "Move to your left, and cross over into the opposite alcove."

Sydney dashed across the corridor and faded back into the next alcove. She heard the sound of the guard's footsteps moving away.

"All right," Noah said. "Now hold on a second because he's between you and the access panel. Just give me a second and . . ."

His voice suddenly rose, and he yelled, "Hey! I told you to wait. Stay where you are."

Sydney shook her head and whispered into the microphone.

"Noah, I haven't moved. I'm right where you told me to be."

"What? But you're right . . . "

There was a terrible pause, and then Noah's voice came back, urgent and on the brink of panic.

"Sydney, I've got multiple bodies on my screen

and they are not museum security, repeat, *not museum security*."

Sydney suddenly heard a crash. At the end of the corridor, the guard's flashlight rolled by, scattering light across the walls. Sydney felt ice run through her veins, and she flattened back against the wall of the alcove.

"What do you want me to do?" she asked, panicked. *They must be Viktor's men.*

"We've gotta get you back to the access panel."

"Is my route clear?"

"It's hard to tell," Noah said, "I can't get a number, they're all dressed the same."

Sydney felt the walls closing in on her. She risked a glance around the corner and saw a masked figure streak past the corridor.

"Okay," Noah said, "Go now. Down the hall, and one alcove over."

Sydney moved, but she was only two steps out into the hall when Noah's voice was back in her ear.

"No, go back. One's headed your way."

She spun and ducked back into the alcove.

"Try the other way," Noah said. "We'll have to circle you around."

Sydney stepped out the opposite way, and walked straight into a punch. The blow slammed her back into the wall. Two paintings crashed to the floor, and Sydney staggered. She went to block a kick but was too slow. It crashed against her stomach, knocking the wind out of her.

"Sydney!" Noah yelled. "Syd—"

His radio went dead. Sydney scrambled to her feet, already running in the opposite direction, but another masked man was there to meet her. She exchanged blows with him, and got the better of him, dropping him onto his back. She sprinted down the hallway, but she was lost. Her memory of the blueprints failed her and she ran aimlessly, sometimes going over the same path twice.

As she raced past an alcove, a man crashed into her, knocking her down. The cord holding the painting cover snapped, and the painting went skidding across the floor. Sydney looked up to see it get scooped up by another man, who then ran down the hall.

Sydney was on her feet and giving chase when she was hammered out of nowhere by a crushing side kick. The kick landed on her ribs, sending bolts of pain down her side, and she flew through the air. She crashed through a pair of glass doors, sending razor-sharp shards of glass everywhere. Her outfit protected her from being badly cut, but the kick left her reeling and struggling for breath.

She looked up to see the men sprinting as a

team back in the direction they had come, the one in the lead carrying the painting. She counted five attackers, but her view was suddenly impeded by a sixth, the one who had kicked her, who lingered to finish the job.

Sydney looked up into a black mask, but she could feel the man's eyes on her. There was a flash from his wrist, and Sydney saw the knife, gleaming steel from a black handle.

The man moved in for the kill. Sydney moved, tried to stand, and heard the crack of glass beneath her. She looked down at the shards that lay about her. With a gloved hand she scooped one up, gripping it like a knife.

The man advanced, his arm arcing out, his blade whistling through the air. Sydney leaned back, but her feet were unsteady, and she didn't move fast enough. The blade sliced through her jacket, and she felt it nick her skin.

Another inch and you'd be bleeding to death, she told herself. *You have to focus, or you're going to die.*

The guard slashed again and she parried the blade away, lashing out at him with her own improvised blade. He ducked and circled away, glass splintering beneath his feet. Sydney circled as well, keeping a safe distance between them.

The guard suddenly moved in, knife slicing the air. Sydney moved to block but was unprepared for what happened next. The guard swung the knife, making contact with her fragile blade. The shard of glass shattered, leaving her with a cracked, useless splinter. Sydney stared at it in horror, the piece no longer than a pocket knife.

The man went for her stomach, meaning to open her all the way to her sternum. As she side-stepped, the man's momentum carried him past her, and she did what she had to do.

She buried the shard of glass beneath his shoulder blade. Part of the glass sliced through Sydney's glove, drawing blood, but the majority glimmered horribly from the guard's back.

A muffled scream escaped his lips, and he reached back, trying to free the weapon from his back. Sydney kicked him, catching him in his lower back and sending him sprawling across the marble stairs near the foot of the door. His knife clattered out of his hand and fell beneath the stairs, out of reach.

Sydney turned and ran, arms pumping as she fled down the hallway. She hoped none of the men had returned to check on their teammate. At each alcove she flinched, imagining a man lunging at her out of the shadows, but they were empty, and she disappeared around the corner.

She flew through a doorway, headed in the direction of the access panel, her escape a mere two rooms away. But as she turned the corner, she cried out. The ceiling panel high above was still open, *but the rope was gone*. There was no way for her to reach the ceiling.

She felt panic overwhelm her when suddenly Noah's head popped out of the panel.

"Come on!" he screamed, and held an arm out to her.

She leaped and his hand gripped her forearm. He pulled her up into the ceiling, her kicking feet clawing at the edge of the hole.

They fled back through the access tunnel, stopping at the security panel. Noah tore the wires from the panel, sending a shower of sparks over his face.

"Are you all right?"

Sydney stripped the mask from her face.

"Yes!" Sydney gasped out. "Why did you pull the rope?"

"I didn't want any of them following you up. Come on."

They scrambled up the ladder and out into the street. In seconds they were in the van, and Noah peeled away from the curb, leaving the cones and traffic horses for someone else to deal with.

"What happened to your radio back there?" Sydney asked.

"I was going to help you," Noah explained. "I ran down the tunnel and one of the wires got stuck on a pipe and it ripped it apart."

He turned to look at her, light flickering on his face as they sped past the streetlamps.

"Are you sure you're all right?" he asked.

Sydney nodded and slumped back in the seat, watching the streets fly by. They returned to the bookstore. Noah pulled the van around back with the headlights off as he maneuvered the van into a parking space. They knocked at the door, and the old woman let them in.

Sydney changed into a pair of worn jeans and a knit top that the woman gave her, and they went down to the basement and contacted Sloane. While they waited, Noah looked at her cut finger and treated it with a first-aid kit that the old woman provided.

He stuck a finger through the hole in the glove.

"It looks like the glove ate most of it, so at least you won't need stitches."

He cleaned the cut with peroxide and taped it, coating the inner bandage with a thin coat of antibiotic.

The computer lit up and Sloane appeared. Sydney was surprised to see that the background was not his office. Gone were the sterile walls and harsh light, replaced by a comfortable chair and a gentler light that softened his features, despite the bags Sydney could see beneath his eyes.

"Good evening, Agent Bristow, Agent Hicks. Please pardon the view. I'm transmitting from a secure connection at my home."

"Is everything all right?" Sydney asked. There was something about him, something in his eyes that concerned Sydney.

"Yes, of course," Sloane said. "My . . . my wife wasn't feeling very well this morning, so I decided to work at home today."

"Oh, please tell her I hope she feels better," Sydney told him. She had met Emily Sloane at a dinner party earlier in the summer and had an immediate connection with her.

Sloane smiled. "Thank you, Sydney. I'm sure she'll be fine."

His expression changed for a moment, and his eyes grew distant while his fingers absently traced the grain of his desk. Then he looked up at them, sitting back in his chair and adopting the more professional demeanor Sydney was used to.

"So how did this evening's mission go?" he asked.

Sydney opened her mouth to speak, but Noah leaned forward and cut her off, his posture almost dismissive of her.

"We lost the package, sir."

Something flickered in Sloane's eyes. His expression went dark, cold.

"And how did that happen?" he asked.

"Keller's guards intercepted us. We had the package, but it was lost."

"Not exactly," Sydney cut in, shooting an apologetic look at a startled Noah for correcting him. Her eyes locked on Sloane. "Yes, it was taken," she said. "But not before I scanned it."

Sloane leaned forward.

"You scanned it at the museum?"

"Yes, sir. I felt it would be a prudent move in the event of something going wrong, which is exactly what happened."

She reached into her bag and withdrew the scanner. She hooked it up to the computer and downloaded the file to Sloane.

"You should be receiving it now." Sydney continued.

"Excellent work, Agent Bristow," Sloane said. "We should be able to decipher the last piece of the puzzle and determine where the secret location is. We have, however, devised a contingency plan, just as you did, in case we're not able to get to the location before Viktor does.

"There should be a box there addressed to Andie Carlino."

There was a box on the table beside the laptop with *Andie Carlino* written across the top.

"Yes," Sydney said, "it's here."

"Open it, please," Sloane said.

Sydney tore the brown mailing paper, revealing the cardboard box inside. She lifted the lid and revealed the Calistrano key.

"You'll need to use the key to open the crypt, secure its contents, and then return to Los Angeles." Sloane paused. "Now, Sydney, what is your schedule for the next couple of days?"

"We have a performance tomorrow evening," Sydney said.

"That's fine," Sloane said, "keep an extra eye on Viktor. Chances are he'll be making a move in the next couple of days if Keller is able to decipher the code."

"I will," Sydney said.

"Very well," Sloane said, "we'll be waiting to hear from both of you, then. Good luck."

Sydney and Noah thanked him and he was gone, the screen going dark. Noah continued to stare at the screen, clearly distracted.

"How does that work?"

Sydney wasn't sure what he meant. Noah was looking at her now, but his eyes were inscrutable.

"How does what work?" she asked, bewildered.

"The show," he said. "Come on, you've got to have some secrets to tell."

She swallowed. She hadn't done anything wrong, not really, but somehow she felt incredibly guilty about all the time she had spent with Trevor.

"What do you mean?" she asked.

He stood up from the chair, his hands digging into the pockets of his jacket.

"I mean it's a magic show. You must have some secrets about how some of those things work."

"Why do you want to know?" she asked, trying to sidestep.

He shrugged. "Just curious," he said.

"They use mirrors, sleight of hand, and radios in the act," she explained.

"Radios?" he asked. "For what?"

"Timing," she responded. "They use them to give us cues and to give us a heads-up about changes and transitions."

"Oh," he said with a smile, "that makes it easier."

Sydney frowned. Just when things were good with Noah, he always said something, made some allusion to her performance that made her feel really insecure. "What exactly does *that* mean?" she asked. "Easier? Oh, I understand. It would have to be easy for me to do it. Is that it?"

Noah blinked in surprise, and his hands slid out of his pockets. "Sydney, come on. That's not—"

"Because I could only do the easy jobs, right? Or did you not notice that *I* was the one Sloane sent in on the museum job. Or maybe you *did,* and that's what's bothering you. He sent me in to do what should have been your job, and I did it. "

"Sydney," Noah said, stepping toward her. Before she knew it, his hands were on her shoulders. "I did notice that you were the one Sloane sent in. That's why I volunteered to be the agent he sent in to work with you." He leaned over and kissed her softly on the lips. "Now, when are you going to wise up?"

Sydney swallowed and stared into Noah's eyes. There was mischief and a little superiority there . . . but there was also deep caring and maybe, even, something more.

She thought of her picnic with Trevor Raven, and suddenly it made her sick to her stomach.

"Right now," she whispered, leaning in to kiss him again. "Right now."

13

"OH, MAN." SYDNEY LET out a groan as she awoke the next morning and tried to sit up. She winced and immediately placed her hand on her side. Her ribs weren't broken, but they were definitely banged up. Slowly, she got out of bed, gingerly testing her range of motion. When she lifted her shirt, she saw the purple bruise that had spread there. There was nothing to do but hope that aspirin would help the pain.

She stepped out into the hallway and padded down the hall, going to get aspirin from her makeup bag. The door of the bathroom was ajar and the light was on. The sink was running, and Sydney could hear movement in the bathroom.

Wow, Angela's up early, she thought, and started to turn back to her room. Something caught her eye and she stopped. She slowly inched her way closer to the bathroom.

Sitting on the top of the closed toilet seat was a towel, a hairbrush, *and a blue arm cast.* She inched closer and looked through the crack on the hinged side of the door.

Angela was bent over the sink, washing her face. She wore only sweatpants and a bra, and Sydney could clearly see the deep cut beneath her shoulder blade. The wound was fresh, and Sydney could see discarded, bloody bandages piled up on the edge of the sink.

As quietly as she could she went back down the hall and into her room, closing the door behind her. Her hand went to her mouth, her eyes wide with terror and confusion.

It was Angela at the museum, Sydney thought. *There were six people at the museum. . . .*

Her mind reeled as details suddenly flooded through it. Six *assistants in the show.* Six *thieves at the museum. I watched Viktor talking with one of the guards who brought him the painting. . . . Wait!* **Brought** *it to him?*

She went through the details of that event. In her mind she went down to the lobby and saw Viktor talking with the guard and then handing the painting back to him.

No, she thought. *Not handing it back to him, giving it to him.* But where did he get it?

And suddenly it all made sense. She should have noticed it the first time. During breakfast, Viktor would always arrive to pick up the cue logs, and Angela would go to her room and bring him the case. The case that held the cue logs *and the painting* she and the other assistants had stolen the night before. Viktor, Angela, and all the other assistants were working together. The guards from the train only worked for Keller. And Trevor was caught in the middle.

There was a soft knock at her door and Sydney nearly jumped out of her skin. She could hear Angela's voice on the other side.

"Nicole, are you awake?"

She saw me, Sydney thought. *No, she didn't. If she saw you, she would have attacked you right there in the hallway.*

Then what does she want?

Sydney would have laughed at the battle of voices in her head if it hadn't been so serious.

She wants to see if you're awake, that's all. And

if you act like anything is out of the ordinary, she's going to suspect you right away, so knock it off.

Sydney put a hand to her eyes and rubbed pretend sleep from them. She fumbled at the handle and opened the door wide to reveal Angela standing on the other side.

The first thing that Sydney noticed was that the cast was back in place over her arm. She had also put a robe on, concealing the scar.

"I'm sorry. Did I wake you up?" she asked.

Sydney yawned and shook her head.

"No, no, I'm fine. What time is it?"

"It's after nine, and I didn't know if you needed to do anything before tonight's show. I'm leaving now. We've got some stuff to do at the theater."

Of course you do, Sydney thought. *You have a painting to analyze.*

"Can I offer you a ride?" Angela said.

"No thanks, I'm good," Sydney said.

"Well then, we'll see you tonight."

Angela walked down the hall, and Sydney heard her bedroom door open and then close. She sat down on the edge of the bed, trying to figure everything out. She needed to go back to the bookstore and contact Sloane.

But wait a minute, she thought. *If I contact Sloane and tell him what's going on, he'll send in reinforcements, probably Noah. And although I would give my eyeteeth to see him again, I should probably be a big girl and do this myself. After all, I've come this far.*

She lay back on the bed, watching the early-morning sunlight move across the ceiling as she ran through her options in her mind.

If they don't know that I was the one at the museum last night, then I'm in no greater danger than I was before, she thought. But if they did, people other than herself were going to get hurt.

She sat up suddenly, and in fifteen minutes she was showered and out the door, heading for the theater.

* * *

"I don't understand," Trevor said. He stared at Sydney, dumbfounded. "You're who . . . what . . . ?"

"I'm sorry," Sydney said. They were in his dressing room, the door securely closed "I know this is hard to understand, and believe me, leaving you in the dark was an option. But I thought it was only right that you should know. Things are starting to get dangerous, and I didn't want you caught in the crossfire."

"Well, what am I supposed to do?" he asked.

"Go on with the show," Sydney explained. "Viktor will undoubtedly be making a move soon, and when he does, we'll take care of it. But if something happens, I want you clear of it, and I thought if you knew the truth then you could step back and let us do our job."

Trevor put his head in his hands.

"Are you okay?" Sydney asked, genuinely concerned.

He looked up, and Sydney could see how pale he was. He cleared his throat and shook his head.

"I just feel like a fool," he said. "Being lied to . . . by so many people."

His eyes flickered to her and then away, and Sydney felt the full weight of her charade come crashing down on her.

"I'm sorry," Sydney said softly, and she meant it.

He sat back in the chair and took a deep breath. "So, can you tell me what Viktor is looking for exactly?"

"The crypt of Calistrano."

Trevor laughed and shook his head.

"It's a fairy tale. It doesn't exist. Calistrano is a myth, right up there with Santa Claus. He's not real."

Sydney slowly reached up and tugged at a cord

around her neck. She pulled the key out from under her shirt and showed it to him.

"But this is real," she said. "I took this from a man who has been working with Viktor. They believe it will open whatever they find at Calistrano's crypt."

Trevor stared at the key, shaking his head in disbelief. "Why did Viktor do this? Why use me like this?"

"The tour," Sydney said. "It provided him the cover story to acquire the pieces that he needed, and the crew that he needed to get them. He could move from city to city and not be suspected. He also had access to your library to do his research."

"My private library?" Trevor said, his eyes wide. "I can't believe it, that son of a . . ."

He laughed again, a defeated, resigned sound. "I guess I'm too trusting."

"That's okay," Sydney said. "I am too." Sydney rose from her chair and went to the door. "I better go."

"Sydney."

She turned back.

"I like that," Trevor said. "I like it better than Nicole."

Sydney went back to the dressing room and

changed into her costume, being careful not to let anyone see the key around her neck.

As she did her makeup, Angela entered the dressing room. She passed out the earpieces to everyone, stopping last at Sydney's table. She was all smiles, no visible sign of the brutal combatant she had been the night before. The cast was back on her arm.

"We're on in ten minutes," Angela said. "Full house."

"Great," Sydney said, smiling brightly.

The show began as it always did, the applause of the audience greeting them warmly. They worked their way through the routines, Trevor stunning the crowd again and again.

Sydney felt distracted, and she struggled to keep her mind focused. At last they came to the grand illusion. Sydney stood in the wings as the lights dimmed and the fog began to roll across the stage. The music began, setting the mood.

Beth and Brianne crossed the stage, pushing the ebony case into place, and the other girls followed, dancing with the dead.

Beth and Brianne moved over to Sydney.

"Are you ready?" Beth whispered, and Sydney nodded.

"Stand by," Angela said through their earpieces.

The girls did another revolution around the stage, and then Angela's voice came back.

"All right, go."

Sydney let Beth and Brianne lead her across the stage to the ebony case. Brianne produced the length of rope and showed it to the audience. She turned to Sydney, who held her wrists out. Brianne tied them, and then she and Beth ushered Sydney into the case, closing the doors and sealing her in the dark.

Trevor's voice began to boom out of the speakers overhead. There was suddenly a soft pop in her earpiece, and Sydney shook her head to clear it as Trevor's voice suddenly spoke to her.

"Sydney, Sydney, Sydney," he said in the earpiece. "It's true, it has a much nicer ring than Nicole."

There was a sudden click on the doors, one she had not heard before. Sydney pushed at them with her hands. The doors were locked.

"I'd like to thank you for being so honest," Trevor continued. "I was wondering just how long it would take for me to win your trust. It actually wasn't as hard as I suspected it would be. You're right, you are too trusting."

He laughed. "Some dinner, wine, and entertainment, and you were like a child, falling for all of it. I do believe you were falling for me. How sweet.

"We didn't think that anyone knew what we were up to, but when the key was taken from the train we knew that someone had found out. And we figured that that same someone—let me guess, the CIA?—would send someone for the rest."

Sydney turned her wrists to free herself from the rope but couldn't. In the dim light she looked down at the knot, and saw that it was tied differently, real knots replacing the fake ones. She looked out through the crack in the door. Beth and Brianne stared at her, their eyes cold beneath their masks. Sydney looked in horror at all the assistants and saw their eyes, all equally cold.

"But you would need an opportunity, wouldn't you?" Trevor continued. "And we gave you one. We faked Angela's injury, and suddenly we needed a new assistant. There were a lot of girls to choose from, but there was something about your resume that didn't seem right. It seemed like an illusion, and I can *always* tell one of those."

Trevor stepped onto the stage, cape billowing out behind him. He wore a mask as well, its harsh, grinning features carved in ivory. It was the face of death. Sydney saw his jaw working beneath the mask as he spoke into a microphone hidden there. There was his voice, theatrical and mysterious, projected overhead; and the voice in her ear, all too real and full of malice.

"And now, thanks to you, we have the key. A fitting end would be for us to simply run you through with the swords, but that would be such a mess to try and explain. Instead, Viktor and Angela are waiting for you downstairs. When the elevator drops, Angela will take your place, and Viktor will deal with you."

He moved to the box and leaned in close. Sydney could see his eyes staring at her. He winked.

"Thanks for everything."

He slid the staff across the door, and the elevator dropped.

PART ONE

14

JUST AS TREVOR HAD said, Angela and Viktor were indeed waiting when the elevator stopped. Angela wore a matching copy of Sydney's costume, and her hair was pulled back in the same style. Viktor held a pistol equipped with a silencer. He grabbed Sydney and hauled her off the platform.

"Wait," Angela said, and Viktor stopped. Angela reached out and slid Sydney's mask off. Then her fist shot out, catching Sydney on the jaw, drawing blood from her lip.

"That was for last night," Angela snarled, and slipped Sydney's mask over her face. She produced a roll of tape and tore a strip off, roughly pasting it across Sydney's lips.

She reached out again and tore away at the neck of Sydney's dress. She yanked the key over Sydney's head and slid the cord over her own, tucking the key beneath her dress. She turned to Viktor.

"Get rid of her." Then she stepped onto the elevator

Viktor grabbed Sydney and dragged her away. The ropes that bound her cut deeper into her wrists. She stumbled and hit the floor with a thud, landing on her bruised ribs. Her scream was muffled by the tape jammed over her mouth.

Her breath came in hitching sobs, and tears welled and ran from her eyes. Viktor's foot dug into her stomach, knocking the wind out of her and savagely rolling her onto her back. She squinted up into the light from the bulb overhead until Viktor stepped over her, casting his shadow across her face.

He pulled the slide on the gun, a bullet snapping into the chamber with a flat crack, and flipped the safety off. He raised the pistol, and despite the backlight, Sydney could see the grin that split his face into a grotesque display of joy. He thumbed the hammer back with a click that echoed painfully in her ears.

"Good-bye, Sydney," he said, and squeezed the trigger.

There were two dull reports, savage explosions dulled by a silencer, and Sydney felt her body go rigid. She felt no pain, but knew it was the shock that had numbed her, spared her from the searing agony that such wounds inflicted.

She let out a shuddering breath, and fresh tears ran down her face. *This is how I'm going to die,* she thought. The world swam before her eyes, darkness creeping in at the edges. She saw spots, and the colors of the world ran wild. The light overhead seemed orange, her blue dress turned green, and Viktor's white shirt was red.

Sydney's ears were suddenly ringing and she squeezed her eyes shut. When she opened them, the ringing subsided and the normal colors of the world had returned.

But Viktor's shirt was still red.

His hand floated up to his chest, the fingers twitching. His knees suddenly buckled, and he crashed to the floor, the gun tumbling from his hand. His face landed inches from Sydney's, and she stared into his dead eyes and the trickles of blood that ran from his nose and mouth.

A figure emerged from the shadows, and Sydney turned to see Noah as he stepped into the light, a silenced pistol gripped in his hand. He dropped to his knees beside her, pulling a knife out of his pocket. With a snap of his wrist the knife flashed opened, the blade gleaming, and he cut the rope at her wrists. He dropped the gun and knife and gently peeled the tape away from her mouth.

"Are you all right?" he asked. But Sydney, through her building haze of pain, could only gaze up at him, speechless.

"Sydney? Sydney?" he asked again. He raised her to a half-sitting position, his arms cradling her. She looked up at him, her eyes swimming in and out of focus.

"Noah?"

He smiled then, a sigh of relief spilling out of him. He wiped a hand across her face, drying the tears on her cheeks.

"Are you okay?" he asked.

"I think so."

"Good, because I need you to get up. Right now."

She looked at him wide-eyed.

"What?"

Suddenly there was the thunder of applause from above them, and Noah pointed toward the ceiling.

"Do you hear that? We're going to have company in about a minute, so I need you to get up *right now*."

He rose to his feet, his arms still under her, and lifted her to a standing position. She wobbled for a moment on shaking legs, and then braced herself against a nearby wall. Noah scooped the gun from Viktor's hand.

"Here, take this," he said, handing it to Sydney.

He slipped his jacket off and draped it over Sydney's shoulders. He bent down and rolled Viktor onto his back.

"What are you doing?" Sydney asked.

He turned and looked up at her. "Was he supposed to do something with you?" he asked.

"What do you mean?"

"After he killed you, was he supposed to get rid of you?"

Sydney froze for a moment. Only moments ago she had thought she was going to die, but to hear it from Noah made it more real than she could have imagined. And she suddenly felt dizzy.

"Sydney!" His voice, sharp and direct, cut through the haze. "Was he supposed to do something with you?" he asked again.

"Yes, he . . . he was supposed to get rid of my body."

"Good."

She looked at him with stunned disbelief.

"Good?" she said. "How is that good?"

"Because if he's gone for a while, they won't miss him. We can't leave him here anyway, or they'll know you're still alive."

With strength Sydney didn't expect from his trim frame, he hoisted Viktor's body over his shoulders as if it were half its weight.

"Come on, we gotta go." He headed for the rear stage door, and Sydney followed.

They crashed out through the door into the alley and headed away from the theater toward a side street. Traffic was light at such a late hour, and the sidewalks were empty.

Noah stole a glance around the corner, and then turned to Sydney.

"Two cars up, stay by my side."

He stepped out onto the sidewalk and Sydney followed close behind. They reached a dark-colored sedan, and Noah raised the pistol.

"Look out," he said, and fired. With the silencer, and out in the open, the gun emitted a low cough, and the rear passenger window of the car instantly spiderwebbed with the sound of breaking ice. He kicked the glass out of the window, clearing the doorframe.

"Open it up, hurry," he said. Sydney quickly popped the lock up and opened the door.

"Pop the trunk," Noah said.

Sydney slid across the rear seat, looking out for broken glass, and hopped into the front. She sat the driver's seat and reached along its base until she found the trunk switch. She lifted it and the trunk popped open.

Quick as a flash, Noah dropped the body of Viktor into the trunk and slammed it shut. He moved around to the driver's side door, and Sydney lifted the lock and slid over to the passenger seat. Noah opened the door and got in, already reaching under the dash. He pulled out a handful of wires and stripped them with his knife. In seconds the engine roared to life and they tore away into the night.

15

THEY ARRIVED AT A small secluded farmhouse on the outskirts of Amsterdam. Noah leaped out and opened the vine-covered gate that barred their entrance. He pulled the car up to a weather-beaten garage, its dilapidated roof pitching precariously to one side. He exited the car again and opened a hidden access panel. He entered a code and the garage door swung up, rattling on its track. The interior of the garage was bathed in red light from the ceiling bulb, and Sydney knew they were in a safe place. The red bulb was designed to light their way without being seen from the road. In the light, Viktor's blood, which was splashed across Noah's shirt, appeared black.

Noah waved to her to pull the car into the garage. She slid over to the driver's seat and slowly drove into the space beside a car covered in a tarp. She killed the engine, and the cooling block ticked loudly in the confined space of the garage. Noah opened the door and held his hand out to her.

"Come on," he said.

She took his hand and let him ease her from the car. He put a sheltering arm around her and let her out into the darkness, a red-lensed flashlight in hand. Behind them the garage door rattled back down, and then they were left with silence.

They walked up a narrow path to the main house, covered with vague shadows in the throw of the flashlight. They got to the door and Noah handed her the flashlight. He slid a hidden panel away on the frame of the door and entered another access code on the numeric panel. There was a bang as the lock retracted, and Noah pushed the door open, revealing the stairs beyond, also lit in red.

They went inside and Noah closed the door behind them. A second later the lock snapped back in place and they went up the stairs.

The interior of the farmhouse was modest, with simple furniture. Noah led her into one of the bedrooms and sat her down on the bed, wrapping the comforter around her.

"Are you okay?" he asked. "Are you warm enough?"

"Yes," she said.

"I want you to lie down for a few minutes," he said. "I'm going to go change and make a call."

And with that he was gone, slowly closing the door behind him. She lay back on the bed, hearing the springs creak beneath her. She didn't think she would actually sleep, but she was out in seconds, and her brief rest was filled with a nightmare.

In it, she was back in the basement of the theater, but Noah wasn't. Viktor, grinning down at her, shot her twice. In the dream the gun didn't have a silencer, and the twin reports were thunder. She went temporarily deaf under the assault, leaving her with only the panicked staccato of her heartbeat roaring in her ears. It slowly began to fade, the silence between beats growing longer and longer.

She felt the two slugs burning red hot in her abdomen, twin needles of pain that began to spread their burning poison through her body. She looked down and saw the widening pool of blood beneath her, its surface a shimmering crimson mirror.

And before she awoke with a scream, she saw

the reflection of Viktor's face in the blood. Then it was her father's face, and he grinned at her.

She awoke and lurched to a sitting position, a scream bubbling over her lips. Noah, who was standing at a nearby dresser with his back to her, spun around and flew to her side.

"Sydney," he said. "You're awake, you're awake."

He gripped her by the shoulders, steadying her. She looked at him with terror-stricken eyes and fell into his arms, which wrapped around her, pulling her close. She hugged him hard, grateful for the voice at her ear.

"You're okay," he whispered, repeating it again and again until her grip relaxed.

She sat back, wiping sweat from her brow. He grabbed a bottle of water off the bedside table and offered it to her. She drank nearly half of it in two swallows, took a breath, and then finished the rest. Noah took the empty bottle and set it on the floor.

"I don't understand," Sydney said slowly. "How did you know?"

"What was going on?" he said. He tapped his ear. "Your earpiece," he continued. "I remembered what you told me about the earpieces you use, so I used the radio kit from the other night to listen in."

"Why?" Sydney asked.

He shrugged. "I was just curious. I wanted to hear what was going on, see how the show worked. I wanted to see you. I'm glad I did too. When I heard Trevor talking to you, I went straight to the basement, and got there just in time."

Sydney opened her mouth to tell him how grateful she was. He had saved her life, coming out of the shadows to rescue her. She suddenly stopped as her heart filled with dawning horror. *Some dinner, wine, and entertainment, and you were like a child, falling for all of it. I do believe you were falling for me. How sweet.*

"Did you . . . did you hear everything Trevor said?"

Something flickered in Noah's eyes, and she knew that he understood what she was talking about.

She felt new tears brimming beneath her eyelids. She looked down, not wanting him to see the tears, and because she couldn't look him in the eyes, into the face of the man who had saved her . . . and really, truly cared for her.

"Sydney."

His voice was soft, comforting. She squeezed her eyes shut, and the tears that had been building there ran down her face in hot streaks.

Noah lifted her face to his, and she reluctantly met his gaze.

"Yes," he continued, "I heard it all. But I've been in the field for a lot longer than you have, Sydney. I know what it's like to get caught up in your mission . . . to start believing that this world that you're dabbling in, this alias that you've created for yourself, is somehow real."

"I feel like such an idiot," Sydney mumbled, wiping her face. "Really, it takes a lot more than dinner to woo me. I definitely require lunch too," she said, trying to make a joke.

"When I heard Trevor tell you that he was going to kill you, I freaked out," Noah went on. "I ran down there, not knowing what I would do if I was too late. I could never live with myself if anything happened to you. You mean—" He cut himself off and ran his fingers through his hair. "But hey, look, I'm not going to pretend that whatever happened with you and Trevor—"

"Nothing happened," she blurted out, needing him to know that more than anything.

Noah pulled her close and she relaxed in his arms, feeling the warmth of his body against her, the touch of his clean black T-shirt against her face.

But then she looked again. He had changed his

pants as well, changing the dress slacks into a pair of black combat fatigues, and his business shoes into black lace-up boots.

"Why are you dressed like that?" she asked.

He stood up and walked to the dresser. He leaned back against it, his muscular arms crossed over his chest.

"While you were sleeping I called Sloane. Keller found the crypt."

"What about our team?" Sydney asked.

"They beat us to it. He must have had a bunch of crews in different spots around the world, because they were there and gone by the time we got there. And another thing, Trevor pulled up stakes."

"What do you mean?" Sydney asked.

"He cancelled the rest of the tour. Claimed there was a family emergency. Everything's been packed up, and they've booked a ferry to London that leaves tonight. And Keller's en route to meet him onboard, presumably with whatever they found in the crypt in tow."

He turned back to the dresser and returned with a handful of neatly folded clothes and a stack of papers, including a passport.

"You have two options," he started. "One is to take these clothes and papers and head back to Los Angeles. The papers will give you a new identity and help you get past any problems should Trevor have people looking for you. You've been through a lot, and Sloane has approved your return. You've done as much as you can."

"And option two?" Sydney asked.

He tossed a duffel bag onto the bed. She unzipped the bag to reveal black combat gear.

"Option two," he said, "is to join me in infiltrating the ferry and recovering the artifact. Know this right now: either way, whether you go or not, I'm going after Trevor."

"Why?" Sydney asked.

Noah crossed his arms across his chest again, and his eyes burned.

"Because he tried to kill my girl, and that wins him a visit from me."

16

UNDER COVER OF DARKNESS, the ferry
surged across the English Channel, ducking in and
out of pockets of fog. Its massive engines stirred
the water with a tremendous roar, which allowed
the unnoticed approach of the tiny speedboat
pulling alongside the ship.

Noah piggybacked the smaller boat to the ferry,
attaching a magnetic tether to the ferry's hull.

Using one of the anchor chains, Sydney and
Noah scaled the side of the ship and dropped onto
the deck, hiding behind a stack of crates.

Noah slid a watertight bag off his back and unloaded their equipment. Each took a pair of night-vision goggles and a radio kit. Noah slid a clip into a silenced pistol and handed it to Sydney.

"No thanks," she said, and slid the radio ear-piece into her ear.

"Hey," Noah said, "take the gun."

"I don't want a gun."

"I'm not asking you, Sydney. I'm *telling* you. I understand your being apprehensive about it, but I can't be worrying about you. . . . These people will kill you Sydney, they've already proven that. If you don't want to use it, that's fine, but you are taking a gun."

He held it out to her again, and she took it, sliding it into the holster at her hip. She picked up a small electronic device.

"What's this?" she asked.

"It's a homing beacon. It's completely water-proof." He flipped a lever and a red light at the top began to flash.

"If you get in trouble, or we need to bail out into the water, hit the switch and the cavalry comes to get you."

He switched it off and clipped it onto his vest. Sydney followed suit. Noah slid his goggles down over his eyes and peeked around a corner of the crates.

After a moment, he whispered, "Sydney, come here."

She crawled over to him, sliding her own goggles on, and the world was lit up in shades of green. Using hand signals, he told her to take a look. She peeked out around the corner.

The main deck of the ferry was filled with the trucks and buses from the show. She looked farther down and saw the two Mercedes sedans, surrounded by three of the guards carrying submachine guns.

They ducked back behind the crates, lifting their goggles.

"What do you think?" Sydney asked.

"It looks like we've got two points to attack," he said. "The guards, and then wherever the key is."

"Angela has the key," Sydney said.

"How do you know?" Noah asked.

"Trust me," Sydney said, remembering Angela showing her the key, "I know."

"Fine," Noah said. "But it's a double-edged sword. If we go for the key first, the guards could come running. If we go for the guards, chances are everyone will know we're coming."

"What about the artifact?" Sydney asked.

"It's in the car," Noah replied.

Now it was Sydney's turn to ask the question.

"How do you know that?" Sydney asked.

"Keller's not in the car, and there are three very heavily armed guards standing around it. The only reason he would divide his security team like that would be to guard something just as valuable as he is. So the artifact must be in one of the cars, and if we don't get the keys, we're going to be in trouble. Those sedans are armored, state-of-the-art tanks. Try to shoot the windows and they'll just laugh at you."

Noah thought it over for a second, going over their options. Finally, he spoke up.

"Okay, we'll double-team the guards first, and then go after the key. If we're quick, no one will be the wiser."

"No," Sydney said. "You go for the guards, and I'll get the key."

Noah arched an eyebrow at her.

"Are you serious?" he asked.

"Yes," Sydney replied. "If we hit them both at once, they're going to have their hands full."

Noah shook his head and laughed.

"Whatever you say, gorgeous."

He leaned forward suddenly and kissed her. His hands went to the small of her back, pulling her in, and she leaned into his embrace, her arms circling his neck. The kiss lasted for a full minute, completely inappropriate in such a place, but longing overwhelmed logic. They finally broke apart and stood up.

"I'm going to fan out," Noah said, "and see if I can find the other three guards before I go at the car."

"Be safe," Sydney said.

"I will. You too."

And with that he was gone, sneaking off into the shadows. Sydney crept along the deck and disappeared into her own patch of darkness.

Sydney moved along the upper deck, ducking in and out of the shadows. She kneeled down in a corner and toggled the switch on her headset.

"Noah, are you there?" she whispered.

A moment later there was a click in her ear, and Noah's voice came through the earpiece.

"Yeah, go ahead."

"Any luck?" she asked.

"No, not yet. I think . . . Wait. Hold on a second."

The radio went silent. Somewhere on the ship, there was the sudden sound of muffled voices, a crash, and then silence. A second later Noah came back on.

"That's two down, four to go," he said. "Any luck on your end?"

"Not yet," Sydney replied. "I'll let you know."

"Copy that," Noah said. "I'll talk to you soon."

Sydney crept along to the upper deck, looking for any sign of Trevor. The deck was empty, and she moved along unimpeded until she reached the port side. A door on the lower deck opened, casting a pillar of light along the floor. Voices followed, and she recognized them immediately as Trevor's and Angela's. Sydney peered over the rail and saw them standing outside one of the cabin doors.

"As soon as we land I want everything off-loaded and put into storage," Trevor said. "You and I will go directly to the house."

"What about Viktor?" Angela asked.

"He'll meet us there. By now Bristow should be dead and buried."

Sydney felt her hands curl into fists. *How wrong they are,* she thought. *But let them think that, that way they'll never expect what's coming.*

"I'm going back in," Trevor said.

"Go ahead," Angela said, "I'm going to have a smoke."

Trevor disappeared back into the hull of the ship, the heavy door closing behind him. Angela stepped to the rail overlooking the churning waters and pulled a pack of cigarettes from her jacket pocket. She lit one, her features shifting in the flickering flame of the lighter, and then dropped the lighter back into her pocket.

Sydney watched as Angela reached a hand beneath the collar of her jacket and pulled out the key, still attached to the leather cord around her neck. Angela admired it for a moment and then slid it back under her jacket collar.

Sydney leaped over the railing, dropping to the deck below. She landed in a coiled spring, and Angela jumped, startled.

Sydney had the advantage, and could have easily knocked her out before she had a chance to move, but she wanted Angela to know who it was. She stood as Angela whirled around, wide-eyed.

"Hi," Sydney said with a smile, and then punched her. The blow took Angela right off her feet, and she slammed to the deck, the cigarette falling from her hand.

"Nice to see you again," Sydney said, and bent to get the key.

Angela's foot shot out, catching Sydney in the ribs, and she sailed back against the wall, cracking the back of her head on the steel surface.

For a moment she saw stars, and then they cleared to reveal Angela's attack. Sydney parried the blows, still stunned, and countered with a vengeance, dropping Angela to one knee from a pair of crushing punches.

"It's not as easy when I'm not tied up, is it?" Sydney asked.

Angela tried to sweep Sydney's leg. She missed, but Sydney's boots slipped on the wet deck, and she went down hard. Angela was on top of her in moments, one hand at Sydney's throat, while the other reached for the gun on Sydney's hip.

"Easier than you think," she growled.

Sydney struggled for breath, her windpipe squeezed in Angela's grip, and tried to fight for the gun. It slid halfway out of the holster as both Sydney and Angela vied for control.

Sydney was starting to black out, and her grip on the gun was weakening, so she let go. Angela's grip on her throat instantly lessened, thinking the battle was won. Sydney struck the crook of Angela's elbow and the vice on her throat fell away. She grabbed Angela's neck in both hands and yanked her down as she snapped her own head upward.

Angela's face collided with the night-vision goggles, shattering them and drawing blood along the bridge of her nose. The gun fell out of her hand and bounced on the deck, and her body went momentarily limp.

Sydney rolled, reaching for the gun, but Angela snapped back to reality, throwing a choke hold around Sydney's throat and scissoring her legs around Sydney's torso.

Sydney reached back and over, trying to grab Angela, but she couldn't reach her. The arm around her neck tightened, and she felt her throat begin to close.

She reached out for the gun. It lay mere inches from her fingers, and she strained to reach it.

But the ship suddenly listed to one side, and Sydney could only watch helplessly as the gun slid father along the deck.

"Good night, Sydney," Angela breathed viciously in her ear, and Sydney began to fade into unconsciousness, the night growing darker.

She suddenly saw movement out of the corner of her eye, and saw Angela's discarded cigarette, pulled by the angle of the ship, go bouncing by, trailing glowing ashes.

In one movement, Sydney snagged the cigarette from the air as it sailed by and dug the burning end into the back of Angela's hand.

Angela screamed as wisps of smoke sprang

from her skin. Her hold on Sydney broke, and Sydney rolled away, coughing, and sprang to her feet. Angela cradled her wounded hand and staggered to a standing position.

Sydney didn't wait for her to recover; she knocked Angela cold with a kick to the head. Angela struck the deck, out for good, and didn't move. Sydney rubbed her throat and ripped the key from Angela's neck. Jerked by the cord, Angela's head snapped up, and then thumped back to the deck one last time.

"Good night, Angela," Sydney said. She stepped over to the gun, scooped it up, and hurried into the shadows.

"Noah, come in," Sydney rasped into the microphone, still rubbing her throat.

"Go ahead," Noah said. "Are you all right?"

"I'm fine," Sydney replied, her voice growing stronger. "Angela's out, and I've got the key."

"Good work. What about Trevor?"

"I couldn't get to him," Sydney said.

"That's fine," Noah said. "Head back to the car, but stay out of sight until I tell you."

Sydney made her way back down to the main deck and hid behind the crates once again. She peeked around a corner at the car. Without the night-vision goggles there was very little to see, but she could clearly make out the three guards who still stood at their watch. She hit the switch on her radio.

"Noah," she whispered, "I'm at the crates."

"Good," he said. "Stand by."

And as Sydney watched, one of the shadows came to life. Noah glided out of the darkness and hit two of the guards before they could even move. Sydney had always been proud of her hand-to-hand combat skills, emerging victorious from a number of skirmishes, but Noah made her look and feel like a rank amateur. His skills were dazzling. He had dispatched the first two guards, and their limp bodies lay on the deck. The third guard attacked, clearly skilled in his own right, but Noah crushed him. Sydney heard a bone break, happy not to know which one it was, and the last guard dropped. It was over in seconds.

"All right Sydney," he said through the headset, "come on out."

Sydney stepped from behind the crates, staying low, and headed over to Noah. He stooped to get the car keys from the nearest fallen guard, and Sydney froze. The last guard appeared behind Noah, raising his rifle.

"Noah!" Sydney screamed.

Noah spun, his hand a blur. Something streaked

through the air in a silver flash. The guard dropped his gun and staggered, staring dumbly at the knife handle that jutted from his chest. He toppled straight back, landing with a crash.

Sydney sprinted across the deck, forgetting about staying out of sight, and nearly ran into Noah.

"Are you all right?" she blurted out.

"I'm fine," Noah said, managing a grin. "Thanks to you. You have the key?"

Sydney held it up. "Right here."

He held up a set of the car keys and jingled them.

"Then let's get the artifact and get out of here."

He was reaching for the car's door handle when a shot rang out. The bullet slammed off the armored roof of the car, and Sydney heard it scream past her head. They both dropped to a crouch as more gunfire erupted from the upper deck. Noah reached out and snagged one of the guard's rifles. He fired a burst over the roof of the car, and the bullets sparked off the railings of the upper deck.

Sydney could see Trevor up on the deck, a gun in his hands. He was joined by the other assistants and members of the boat crew, all armed to the teeth. More bullets pinged off the car, and Sydney reached out to snag a rifle of her own.

As she did, she saw movement at the end of the

deck. In front of the sedan were four or five trucks parked in a straight line. At the head of the first one, Sydney saw shadows massing.

"Noah!" she screamed, and his eyes followed hers.

He hit a button on the remote attached to the key chain and the car doors unlocked, the dome light flooding the interior. He reached out and yanked the door open a second before two men popped around the front of the truck, guns blazing.

The bullets slammed off the open door as Sydney and Noah ducked behind it for cover. The bullets ricocheted, slicing through the driver's-side tires of the truck in front of them. They exploded, and the truck leaned heavily over the ruined tires. Sydney could smell gasoline, and she saw that the fuel tank had been ruptured. Gas spilled out onto the deck of the ship.

More shots from the upper deck rang past them.

"Get in!" Noah yelled, and returned fire.

Sydney threw herself into the car, hopping over the driver's console into the passenger seat. In seconds Noah was next to her, sliding behind the wheel and slamming the door behind him.

Bullets banged off Sydney's window and she flinched. She turned to Noah.

"Now what?" she asked.

Noah seemed not to hear her, and just looked around at the unfolding chaos.

"Noah? Now what are we going to do?"

"I'm thinking." He looked over into the backseat, then slid his cargo bag off his shoulders. He opened it and pulled out another waterproof weapons bag.

"You have your locator?" he asked.

Sydney pulled it out of her vest pocket and held it up.

"Good," he said. "Activate it."

Sydney popped the top and hit the switch. The red light started blinking, and the activator emitted a high-pitched beep.

Noah pointed to the backseat and handed her the bag.

"Put that in there," he directed.

Sydney leaned over the backseat and saw an incredibly old wooden box. Its surface was covered with elaborate designs identical to the ones on the key.

"Hurry up," Noah barked.

She opened the bag and slid the box into it as more bullets bounced off the car. Noah turned on his own locator and handed it to Sydney.

"Toss this in the bag as well and seal it up."

She dropped the locator into the bag and zipped

it shut. As she tuned back around in the seat, Noah started the car.

"What are you doing?" Sydney asked.

Noah turned and looked at her.

"Hold on," he said.

He slid the transmission lever into reverse and stomped down on the gas pedal. The engine roared and the car lurched backward, colliding with the sedan behind it and driving it back about a foot.

Noah slid the gearshift into drive and the car surged forward, bumping the truck in front of them.

As Noah dropped it back into reverse, the boat suddenly pitched hard to the left. Sydney was thrown across the seat and she slammed into Noah as he hit the gas. He lost his grip on the wheel and the car careened straight back into the other car.

"Sorry," she said. She pushed herself back across the seat and reached for her seat belt.

"No!" Noah yelled. "Don't put that on."

Her hand froze on the strap. "Why?" she asked.

The car drove forward and Noah turned the wheel sharply to the left, but there wasn't enough clearance, and the front right fender banged into the truck. As Noah backed up for the last time, bullets still hailing off the car, he turned to Sydney.

"After we clear the gate, open the door and jump as far away from the car as you can."

Sydney looked at him as if he were speaking one of the few languages she *didn't* understand.

"What do you mean, *jump*?" she asked, her voice high and strained.

"Honey," he said, his voice the definition of calm, "we're going to have to talk about this later. For right now, *please,* just do as I ask."

He hit the gas, and the car flew forward. He yanked the wheel to the left, and the bumper cleared the truck. But the lane was narrow and the car slammed into the side rail, and it buckled in a scream of metal. The rear end of the car teetered out over the water, one tire spinning uselessly in the air while the other screamed for purchase on the slick deck.

And at that moment the boat listed again, heaving heavily to the left. The car leaned farther out, the smoking tire lifting off the deck. Sydney began to slide over toward Noah.

"Stay over there," he yelled. "If both of us are over here, the car will flip over the side."

Sydney grabbed the door handle and pulled herself back over, and the car balanced precariously on the edge of the deck. Sydney looked up.

"Oh no."

The truck began to tip, the passenger side wheels coming completely off the ground, and streams of pouring gas spilling off the boat.

The ferry leaned back to the right in a swell, righting itself. The car shifted, the tire touching down on the deck again. But the mass of the truck was too much, and it began to tip over.

"Noah!" Sydney screamed.

"Hold on!" Noah said, and hit the accelerator.

The tire gripped the deck and the car bolted forward, free of the rails. Sydney watched in horror as the shadow of the falling truck loomed over them, filling the windshield. The car shot underneath the truck, and a second later it crashed to the deck.

The metal crumpled and sparked, igniting the fuel along the deck. A moment later the gas tank exploded. The shock wave blasted out the windows of every vehicle on the deck. The rear window of the Mercedes blew inward and showered Sydney and Noah with shards of glass. A fireball swept the deck, engulfing the cars and trucks.

The car raced down the lane toward the gate.

"Get ready," Noah said. He reached out and grabbed her hand, squeezing it. She squeezed back, her other hand clutching the door handle.

The car crashed through the gate and sailed out over the water. Sydney and Noah opened their doors and jumped, their bodies spinning out and away from the boat.

The car flipped, tires spinning and engine

screaming, and plunged into the water. Sydney and Noah landed several feel from it, the waves swallowing them.

Sydney rose to the surface, coughing out the icy water that had invaded her lungs. She looked over and saw the car filling with water. She kicked to say afloat, still coughing, and lurched forward, paddling furiously toward the car.

She heard Noah calling her, but she swam on, trying to close the distance between her and the car. She was ten feet away when she felt a hand grab her. She spun and looked into the face of Noah.

"What are you doing?" he yelled breathlessly.

"The artifact," she screamed. "It's still in the car."

She tried to pull away but Noah held her fast.

"Sydney, stop. You have to work on staying afloat."

"But the artifact," she cried, fatigue beginning to claim her.

"The locator," Noah breathed.

Sydney stopped struggling.

"They can find it with the locator," Noah continued.

Sydney turned and watched the car disappear beneath the surface, the red glow of its taillights fading as it plummeted to the abyss.

"Come on," Noah said, "we need to—"

Bullets suddenly sliced into the water around them, the thunder of gunfire high overhead. Sydney looked up to see Trevor and the rest of the crew lined up on the deck, all of them firing rifles.

"Go under," Noah said, and they dived deep.

They swam away, the muffled pops of gunfire still chasing them, the bullets leaving trails of bubbles. And then Noah was hit, a bullet cutting across his shoulder.

He started to sink, trailing blood and air. Sydney hooked an arm underneath him and kicked. They bobbed out of the water, coughing, and Sydney heard the clicks of gun magazines being locked in place. She stared forlornly as the shooters took aim.

The deck of the ferry was suddenly awash in brilliant white light, and the roar of a helicopter filled the air. And then there was noise and light all around them as half a dozen ships, drawn by Sydney's locator, appeared out of the dark. Sydney heard voices over loudspeakers telling the ship to stop and the shooters to drop their guns. Overwhelmed and outgunned, the shooters dropped their guns and raised their hands.

Trevor, backlit by the fire from the burning truck, stared down at her, right through her, his eyes filled with hate. He suddenly spun away from the railing and ran back toward the cabin, disappearing from view.

A small boat pulled alongside Sydney and Noah, and she grabbed the outstretched hand of one of the officers reaching for them. They were pulled onto the deck, finally safe.

17

ON A DOCK ON the English side of the channel, Sydney watched as the ferry was tugged in to shore. The fire was out, but smoke still drifted from the deck, mingling with the rising fog.

Noah sat beside her, and she held his hand. They were both wrapped in blankets, and a doctor was stitching the tear along Noah's shoulder. Noah had elected not to go to the hospital. He wanted to be there with Sydney when the ship was brought in.

The ferry stopped at the dock, and the tugboat's motors wound down. The gate, or what was left of it, was swung open, and the occupants were led along the deck by armed guards. Sydney watched everyone go by, their hands cuffed. And though she would be hesitant to admit it aloud, she was deeply satisfied watching Angela get wheeled by on a gurney.

A man in a dark overcoat approached them and showed them his badge.

"Agents Bristow and Hicks, I'm Special Agent Alexander. How are you guys feeling?"

"We're fine," Noah said. "Just another scar for my collection. What about the car?"

"We're scrambling a deep-sea dive as we speak. That was a smart move to put the locator in with the artifact. We should have no problem retrieving it."

The doctor finished stitching Noah's arm and packed up his kit.

"Try and keep it mobile," the doctor said. "In a week or so, you'll be as good as new."

"Thanks, Doc," Noah said, and slid his sleeve back up over the bandage, as the doctor walked away.

Sydney continued to watch as everyone was loaded off the ferry. She suddenly turned to Agent Alexander.

"Wait a minute," she said. "Where's Trevor?"

Alexander turned to her and shrugged.

"He vanished," he said. "We've searched the ship from top to bottom. He's gone."

"How could he be gone?" Noah asked. "The ship was in the middle of the water, and it was completely surrounded. Where could he go?"

"Our boat," Sydney said. "He must have taken our boat."

Alexander shook his head.

"No, it's still there. I don't know how he did it, but he pulled a vanishing act on us. It's kind of fitting, I guess, given his reputation."

"All that work," Noah said, "and the guy gets away."

"I'm sure he'll surface again somewhere," Alexander said. "For now we work on getting the artifact back from the bottom of the channel."

"You'll need this," Sydney said, and handed him the key from her pocket.

Alexander took it, looked at it for a moment, and slid it into his pocket.

"Thanks," he said. "We have clean clothes for you guys at the safe house in London, along with some paperwork. You both have a flight to Los Angeles later out of Heathrow. You want a ride?"

"No thanks," Noah said. "We're good."

"Then I'll see you guys in L.A.," Alexander said, and walked away, leaving Sydney and Noah alone.

"*Why* didn't we take the ride?" Sydney asked.

Noah smiled and pointed to the horizon, which was beginning to brighten.

"I thought we could take a walk and watch the sunrise," he said. "Just the two of us." He stood and let the blanket fall to the ground. "Are you dry enough?"

"Mmm-hmm," Sydney said, letting the blanket slip from her shoulders.

Noah picked up the pair of bright red parkas the paramedics had given them. He helped Sydney put hers on and tried to put on his own but winced as he tried to slide it over his shoulder. Sydney helped him.

"You didn't learn any magic tricks that could help out a wounded guy, did you?" Noah asked hopefully.

Sydney gave his good arm a light punch. "Never, ever talk about magic around me again, thank you very much."

Unless, of course, he was talking about the magical spark that existed between them.

Noah could talk about that anytime.

EPILOGUE

ARVIN SLOANE SAT ALONE at his desk. At this hour, the surrounding offices were dark, the hallways empty and silent. He stared absently at his computer screen, his fingers rubbing the stubble along his chin.

After a moment, his eyes fell to the framed picture on his desk. He smiled, and reached out to change the angle of the picture so he could see it better in the dim light. Emily, his beautiful, loving wife, smiled at him from the picture. The photo had been taken the past summer, a candid shot of her working in the garden of their home that she loved so much.

She kneeled beside a glorious rosebush, its blooms the deepest crimson. There was dirt on her hands, a tiny smudge of it across her cheek, but the light of her smile made it almost invisible. And the roses, as exquisite as they were, paled in comparison to her beauty.

Sloane was lost in her eyes, and in the memory of that day, when the computer suddenly beeped, the screen brightening.

He turned from the picture, his bright daydream drifting into shadow, and faced the screen. He interlaced his fingers, resting his elbows on the desk, and waited.

The cursor blinked, then began to move.

INCOMING REPORT. SECURITY CLEARANCE: LEVEL 1

DIVE SUCCESSFUL. ARTIFACT RECOVERED FROM CAR.

OUR FINDINGS IN REGARDS TO YOUR INQUIRY ARE AS FOLLOWS:

AFTER EXHAUSTIVE STUDY, IT IS OUR CONCLUSION THAT THE ARTIFACT OF VINCENZO CALISTRANO BEARS A SIGNIFICANT RESEMBLANCE TO THE WORK IN OUR PREVIOUS RESEARCH.

FURTHER STUDY HAS INDICATED VINCENZO CALISTRANO WAS INDEED A DISCIPLE AND APPRENTICE OF ONE MILO RAMBALDI.

ALL FINDINGS WILL BE SUBMITTED TO YOUR ARCHIVES.

* * *

Sloane shut the monitor off and sat back in his chair. Only moments before he had been reflecting on the past. Now his mind rushed onward with frightening force, driven by the satisfaction of uncovering yet another piece in the puzzle that was rapidly becoming his obsession.